a little harmless addiction

THE ORIGINAL HARMLESS FIVE
BOOK FIVE

MELISSA SCHROEDER

COVER ART BY
SCOTT CARPENTER

HARMLESS PUBLISHING

contents

also by melissa schroeder

THE HARMLESS WORLD

The Original Harmless Five

- A Little Harmless Sex
- A Little Harmless Pleasure
- A Little Harmless Obsession
- A Little Harmless Lie
- A Little Harmless Addiction

Rough 'n Ready

- Rough Submission
- Rough Fascination
- Rough Fantasy
- Rough Ride

Harmless Trouble

- Harmless Secrets
- Harmless Revenge
- Harmless Scandals

The Wulf Family

- Faith

- Taboo
- Trust

A Little Harmless Military Romance

- Infatuation
- Possession
- Surrender

Task Force Hawaii

- Seductive Reasoning
- Hostile Desires
- Constant Craving
- Tangled Passions
- Wicked Temptations
- Twisted Emotions-coming 2025

THE CAMOS AND CUPCAKES WORLD

Camos and Cupcakes

- Delicious
- Luscious
- Scrumptious

The Fillmore Siblings

- Hate to Love You
- Love to Hate You

Juniper Springs

- Wild Love
- Crazy Love
- Last Love
- Imperfect Love

THE SANTINI WORLD

The Santinis

- Leonardo
- Marco
- Gianni
- Vicente
- A Santini Christmas
- A Santini in Love
- Falling for a Santini
- One Night with a Santini
- A Santini Takes the Fall
- A Santini's Heart
- Loving a Santini

Semper Fi Marines

- Tease Me
- Tempt Me
- Touch Me

The Fitzpatricks

- Chances Are

THE MELISSA SCHROEDER INSTALOVE COLLECTION

Dominion Rockstar Romance

- Undeniable
- Unpredictable
- Unexpected
- Tempted

Mafia Sisters

- Stealing Destiny
- Guarding Fable

Faking It

- Faking it with my Billionaire Boss
- Faking it with my Brother's Best Friend
- Faking it with my Frenemy

The Fighting Sullivans

- Falling for the General's Daughter
- Falling for the Girl Next Door
- Falling for my Best Friend
- Falling for my Baby Mama

Also Included

- Kiss my Tinsel
- Dad Bod Rockstar

Texas Temptations

- Conquering India
- Delilah's Downfall

Hawaiian Holidays

- Mele Kalikimaka, Baby
- Sex on the Beach
- Getting Lei'd

Once Upon an Accident

- The Accidental Countess
- Lessons in Seduction
- The Spy Who Loved Her

The Cursed Clan

- Callum
- Angus
- Logan
- Fletcher
- Anice

The Sweet Shoppe

- Tempting Prudence
- Cowboy Up
- Her Wicked Warrior

By Blood

- Desire by Blood
- Seduction by Blood

Hands On

- The Hired Hand
- Hands on Training

Telepathic Cravings

- Voices Carry
- Lost in Emotion
- Hard Habit to Break

Bounty Hunters, Inc

- For Love or Honor
- Sinner's Delight

Saints and Sinners

- Seducing the Saint
- Hunting Mila

Lonestar Wolf Pack

- Primal Instincts

Texas Heat

- Scorched

Spies, Lies, and Alibis

- The Boss

SINGLE TITLES

- A Calculated Seduction
- Chasing Luck
- Going for Eight

- Grace Under Pressure
- Operation Love
- Saving Thea
- Snowbound Seduction
- Sweet Patience
- The Last Detail
- The Seduction of Widow McEwan

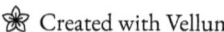

hawaiian terms

Aloha - Hello, goodbye, love
Bra-Bro
Bruddah- brother, term of endearment
Haole-Newcomer to the islands
Howzit - How is it going?
Kamaʻāina-Local to the islands
Mahalo-Thank you
Malasadas- A Portuguese donut without a hole which started out as a tradition for Shrove (Fat) Tuesday. They are deep fried, dipped in sugar or cinnamon and sugar. In other words, it is a decadent treat every person must try when they go to Hawaii. If you do not try it, you fail. Do yourself a favor. Go to Leonard's and buy one. You are welcome.
Pupule - crazy
Slippahs - slippers, AKA sandals

hawaiian terms

Aloha - Hello, goodbye, love
Bra-Bro
Bruddah- brother, term of endearment
Haole-Newcomer to the islands
Howzit - How is it going?
Kamaʻāina-Local to the islands
Mahalo-Thank you
Malasadas- A Portuguese donut without a hole which started out as a tradition for Shrove (Fat) Tuesday. They are deep fried, dipped in sugar or cinnamon and sugar. In other words, it is a decadent treat every person must try when they go to Hawaii. If you do not try it, you fail. Do yourself a favor. Go to Leonard's and buy one. You are welcome.
Pupule - crazy
Slippahs - slippers, AKA sandals

dear reader

We have arrived at the end of the Original Harmless Five. This was also the last book in the Harmless World before I went out on my own into indie publishing in 2011.

The diner mentioned was built around the idea of the old Wailana Coffee House that closed in 2018 after over 40 years in business. And while some things have changed in Honolulu since I have written the books (it was written and edited in 2010 originally) the spirit of the islands stays constant.

I hope you enjoy this new version with the entirely new epilogue for you to enjoy!

Mel

Jocelyn Dupree smiled as her brother showed her around her soon-to-be sister-in-law's house.

"Now the kitchen is in here."

She shared a smile with Cynthia. "Yeah, you don't say?"

"I know it's small compared to your house in Atlanta, but things are smaller here because of the space issue. There is a lot of counter space. I was even thinking of getting Evan to give me an estimate about redoing the area."

"Really?" Cynthia said as she leaned closer to Jocelyn. "That's the first I heard of it."

He tossed her a look then smiled at Jocelyn. If she hadn't missed her brother so much, Jocelyn would have been irritated with his behavior. There was a tiny part of her that wanted to be the biggest bitch on the face of the earth just to see if he would keep smiling at her that way.

"I just thought it might be a good idea. You know, if you decide to stay. You need a bigger kitchen. More professional."

She nodded as she started to walk around the tiny house. A year ago, something like this would have driven her insane. The place she had shared with Mike in Atlanta had been enormous. It had also sported a world-class kitchen with a six-burner Viking and a double oven. God, she missed that kitchen. Sadly, she missed it more than Mike. It probably didn't say that much about the relationship that she longed for her Viking stove more than the man she'd lived with for over a year. With effort, she pushed aside those ideas.

She tucked her tongue in her cheek. "Not sure I'd want you redoing the kitchen right now. Seeing that I just got here. It would be kind of a pain to do without a kitchen."

"Evan would do it really fast."

She didn't say anything as she wandered through the kitchen. She was pretty sure that her brother's best friend had no idea he had just offered up his contracting services. Evan was always in demand thanks to word of mouth, so Jocelyn assumed he would be booked out for months.

That being said, she knew she could probably get a new convertible out of her brother right now. He was ready to do anything to make her feel at home, and if he'd acted like this when she had been a teenager, she definitely would have used it against him. But now, it just amused her, and at the same time, it warmed her heart.

The house was a bit like a doll house. The walls were painted a soft green, with the ceiling off-white. The Koa wood floors gleamed and creaked under her feet as she stepped. It was smaller than she was used to, but she had the strangest feeling, as if she had arrived home. Warmth filled every corner and pulled at her. Here, she would be able to live. Here, she would feel safe.

"Of course, if you don't like that idea, we can find you somewhere else to live."

She thought she heard Cynthia groan, so Jocelyn took pity on her brother—and Cynthia. Truthfully, she was afraid her future sister-in-law might beat him if he kept it up.

"I think maybe I should be here for at least a day before I start coming up with ways to redecorate Cynthia's house. Or plan any major reconstruction," she said with a laugh.

Chris went on as though she hadn't spoken. "Well, if you come on through here, you can see the hallway leads to the bedroom."

"Really?" she asked, her voice heavy with sarcasm.

He glanced at her, and his lips quirked. "I'm just trying to show you around."

She snorted as she leaned against the doorjamb. "It's about fourteen hundred square feet. I think I can find my way around the house, Chris."

His smile broadened, and her nerves settled. "Fine. But if you can't find the bathroom, don't call me in the middle of the night. My woman has me up early to get her to the bakery."

Cynthia laughed. "I can get myself to the bakery just fine. You're the one who insists."

He walked toward the two of them with a concerned look. "I just wanted to make sure you were all set."

There it was again. The look, the tone of voice, the things that told her he didn't trust her alone. Because of one bastard of a boss, she had lost all standing within her family. It was as if she were sixteen years old again, and he caught her hanging out on Bourbon Street with her friends. The logical part of her knew that he had a reason. Even if it wasn't her fault, she understood. Still, it was getting damned old. Worse, she hadn't dealt with that look for over a decade. She was responsible.

"I'm fine. Go. My flight was late, and I know Cynthia gets

up at three in the morning. Plus, I'm exhausted. The trip over was so long from Atlanta."

He crossed his arms over his broad chest. "But what about dinner?"

"Cynthia said there was bread, coffee, and peanut butter. I'm set for tonight."

He hesitated. Irritation swept through Jocelyn. All her brothers had been bad, but Chris had acted odd since she'd arrived. She wasn't a danger to herself. Dr. Sawyer had never deemed Jocelyn a risk for suicide. It had just been physical and mental exhaustion. But she knew that her family saw it differently, especially Chris. Just like she knew he didn't want to leave her alone, he knew there was no way out of it at the moment.

"I'll just be outside," Cynthia said softly as she escaped, leaving Jocelyn to contend with Chris.

She watched the front screen door close before she forced herself to look at Chris. She loved this man. He had been more of a father figure than a brother. In recent years, he hadn't been so bad, but as she watched the worried expression move over his features, she knew she had lost some ground in his opinion. And she knew the look settling on his face. He wanted to have a discussion. Lord, she couldn't handle another talk about her condition.

"I thought you might need someone around," he said.

The urge to scream tickled the back of her throat. "I can handle myself, Chris. I did back in Atlanta. I can do it here."

If she hadn't been watching him so closely, she would have missed the tightening of his jaw. "I'm sorry."

She sighed. "Oh, Chris, I wasn't blaming you. I didn't want you there. What I meant was after. I did that by myself.

Without Mike, you or Mama. I can do this. Don't treat me like I snuck out during Mardi Gras."

"Which you did more than once," he said with a chuckle. He pulled her in his arms and hugged her. "You know I'm just trying to look out for you."

She gave into the need to feel his arms around her, the security she could always count on. From the time their father died, he had been there. He had guided her, helped her pay for culinary school and supported everything she had ever attempted. And in this, she knew that he was on the one real thing in her life.

She pulled back and smiled up at him.

"I know. I can handle myself."

The look he gave her told her he wasn't too sure of it. And she couldn't blame him considering the circumstances she'd been in nine months earlier. Still, it didn't make it any easier to admit that she had to earn his trust again. Especially when it wasn't her fault to begin with.

"Okay." He gave her another quick squeeze. "I'm only a phone call away. And you have Evan's phone number right?"

She nodded. "Don't worry, you got me covered."

She walked him to the door.

"I'm happy you're here, Jocey."

She smiled at his childhood name for her. "I am, too. Now go. Cynthia has an early morning."

He jogged down the path to the car where Cynthia waited for him. With a smile and a wave, he slipped into the car, and she watched the taillights disappear into the Hawaiian night.

She shut the door, locked it, then leaned against it and closed her eyes. For the first time in months, she was alone. All alone. The months in Atlanta she had been partially alone, but not in a real sense. Her mother, her brothers and sister, and the memories had all been there to gnaw at her. She opened her eyes and let the knowledge that she was on her own again settle. Nerves had her stomach tightening, but she smiled as she opened her eyes. She was on her own again.

She walked through the house, a cottage really, and tried to gauge how she would handle tonight. She knew she would handle it just fine, but it wouldn't be easy. Or maybe it would. In Hawaii, she was far away from Atlanta and the memories of Mike and the house they had shared. And she was far away from Greg. She no longer would have to wonder if every little sound was her former boss showing up to finish the assault he had started months earlier. She closed her eyes and pulled in a deep breath, using the breathing exercises her therapist had taught her. After a moment, her heart rate slowed and her panic eased as she opened her eyes.

First thing, she thought as she glanced at her luggage, was to unpack. With more energy than she knew she had, she delved into unpacking her clothes and personal items. Cynthia had moved all of her things to Chris's house in Hawaii Kai, but had left the furniture. Jocelyn loved the look. It had been Cynthia's grandmother's cottage and many of the furnishings were antiques. And Jocelyn thought as she placed some of her shirts into the dresser, definitely Hawaiian. It had been built in the 1930's. And while it had been remodeled over the years, Jocelyn loved that they hadn't gutted the Hawaiian feel.

Less than thirty minutes later, she was done. She glanced around the bedroom when she was done and smiled. The queen-sized bed was covered by a bright Hawaiian quilt and with lots of pillows. It looked so comfortable that she wanted to just collapse on it. Over eleven hours of travel had taken its toll on Jocelyn. But something pushed her out of the room the moment she thought of being alone on that bed. With a sigh, she walked out into the little living room. Now what? It was odd that she would have longed for this day for so long, but now that it was here she didn't know what to do with herself. Usually, she would do some baking to get rid of nervous energy, but she wasn't sure if Cynthia had done any shopping of that kind.

After a little rummaging she found the makings of sugar cookies and started to work. She should have known Cynthia would have had some things ready for her. A fellow baker, they both used baking to console themselves, to forget men, and well, to keep themselves busy. She pulled out what she needed and got to work.

KAI CURSED HIS SISTER. The woman was a pain in the ass. Always had been, always would be. People wondered why he had never had a serious relationship. All they had to do was look at the crazy woman he had grown up with and, until a few months ago, lived with. She drove him insane. No matter how many times he said he wouldn't do what she wanted, here he was driving out to Cynthia's old house to drop off a welcome package for Chris's sister.

Oh, he could have argued with her, but with May, he had figured out years ago to just do what she wanted.

With a sigh, he parked in front of the house and grabbed the basket out of the front seat. He slammed his car door shut and noticed the lights flooding the front lawn. Damn. He was hoping to just leave it in the kitchen and head back home. He was pretty sure that Chris would have taken his sister out for dinner. But apparently, from the music he heard drifting out the windows, he hadn't. He could just make out Brother Iz's voice as he sang about places over the rainbow by the time he made it to the porch. Along with the music, the scent of vanilla and butter mixed in with the plumeria.

He knocked on the door and waited. The music lowered and he heard light steps over the wooden floor.

"Yes?"

"Joceyln? I'm Kai Aiona, May's brother. She sent me over with a basket for you."

She opened the door, the chain still firmly in place. He could barely make her out through the crack of the door. Her green gaze moved down his body then back up, as if she were checking for weapons.

"You say you're May's brother? I thought you were in college." Suspicion clouded her voice.

Irritation boiled in his gut, and he ground his teeth together. Dammit, he wasn't in the mood for a woman from the big city who was afraid of her own shadow.

"That's Danny. I'm Kai, the older one who is thinking very seriously of beating May." He held up the basket. "May thought you would be out and gave me keys to get in. I think she wanted to surprise you."

Her eyes softened and he ignored the jolt in his chest. She closed the door and pulled the chain free. When she pulled the door open, he found himself absolutely and positively stunned.

Soft brown skin, brilliant green eyes surrounded by a wealth of lashes and a full, red mouth. It was all he could see. The woman was gorgeous. She kept her hair short, which accented her high cheekbones. As he allowed his gaze to travel down her body, he felt his heart stop. She was tall, mostly leg, with small pert breasts, and from the shape of her hips, a nice round backside. Oh, Lord, the woman was a goddess.

When he reached her face again, she was frowning. For a moment or two, he couldn't truly think. Those eyes just about did him in. They were exotic, tipped up at the corners.

"You said you had a basket?"

He lifted the basket, still a little taken aback by the woman standing in front of him. That didn't happen to him that often. As a man who ran is own tour company, he had women on his boat a lot. Haoles looking for a good time, and a lot of them gorgeous. They didn't even come close to the woman standing in front of him.

She smiled then and stepped back to allow him to walk through the door. It took him a second or two before he could get his feet to cooperate with him. By the time he did, she was looking at him strangely again. He couldn't blame the woman. He was acting like an idiot without a lick of sense.

"Sorry to bother you. May thought that you might be out to dinner with Chris."

"Chris wanted to. In fact, I think he wanted to drag me to Dupree's and introduce me to everyone he knows in Hawaii." Her voice was filled with enough sisterly affection that Kai knew she loved her brother. "The truth is, it was a hellacious day of traveling."

He offered her the basket and noticed that she did everything in her power not to touch him. And she left the door open. There was a screen there, but he thought it odd that she kept glancing out as if she wanted to assure herself she was safe.

"Yeah, well, May was really worried that you needed that tonight."

"And she badgered you until you brought it." New Orleans threaded her voice. It was deep, sensual, and completely at odds with the person in front of him. She looked the part, but there was the way she held herself. As if she didn't want to be touched, talked to, or bothered.

"Yeah, well, you know how little sisters can be."

She laughed then. The short, sweet sound had his libido dancing.

"Yeah, I do, especially since I figure if it was the other way around, I would be May and you would be Chris," Jocelyn said.

He laughed. "You have her phone number to report that I dropped it off?"

She nodded. "Afraid of her?"

"My father didn't raise an idiot."

They stood like that for a moment or two, the odd silence filling the air around them.

"Well, I guess I should let you get back to..." He glanced in the kitchen. "You just got here and you're baking?"

A light blush stained her cheeks. How she looked so adorable and sexy at the same time. Kai didn't know, but she achieved it somehow. "I'm little out of sorts. Thought I would work off some nervous energy."

"Well, I hope you enjoy the goodies. I'll see you around."

She set the basket on the small kitchenette table. "Oh, please, could you take some of these cookies home?"

Without waiting for an answer, she hurried into the kitchen. He followed her, but not too closely. He apparently made the woman nervous, and she was offering free cookies. He didn't want to miss out on that especially as the smell grew the closer he got to the kitchen.

She was sealing up a plastic baggie by the time he reached the entrance. She handed them to him.

"Thanks again for bringing the basket all the way out here."

"No problem." He turned to leave then stopped. "You wouldn't be interested in going out to dinner would you?"

A look of something akin to panic moved over her face before she hid it behind a mask. "I just got here, so I am not really sure..."

"I understand."

"No. It's...I just got out of a really, really bad relationship. I can't..." She closed her eyes and pulled herself together. When she opened her eyes, he saw regret and embarrassment. "I just don't think I am ready for a date of any sort."

"No problem."

By the time Kai was on his way back down H-3 he realized there was something really off about Chris's sister. She had been through a bad break up, but there was more to it than that. There were women who wanted nothing to do with the locals. Of course, it could just be that soured relationship. And that made her off-limits. He was sick of being the guy who helped women through breakups. The last one had left him bloodied and a little bit more cynical. He definitely wanted to make sure to avoid any woman who was trying to mend a broken heart.

With that, he punched the gas and headed into Honolulu. He had an early morning.

JOCELYN WENT through the basket trying to ignore the fact she had made an idiot of herself. God, did she have to act like the frightened little kitten that couldn't take care of herself? It was embarrassing. Where was Queen Jocelyn, the head bakery chef who scared the hell out of the lower staff members?

She'd turned into a crumbling mess in Atlanta, that's where.

She closed her eyes and held herself in check. She would not cry. It was her first night in Hawaii. The first night of the rest of her life. Greg wasn't here, wouldn't be here. He couldn't hurt her. And dammit, she refused to let the memory of what he had done to her ruin her first night.

The first real interaction with a man, and she'd acted like a virgin, afraid to even touch him. Hell, she had been scared to let him in the house. Even after she knew who he was, remembered May mentioning him, she had been frightened.

He wasn't as tall as Greg. He'd been just an inch or two over her five-foot-eight frame. But he was big. What was it that May had said he did...worked on the docks. And it showed. Sinewy muscles and an alertness that told her he watched everything around him. Oh, he gave off the vibe of a lazy guy, but that was the deception. Her brother Malachi was like that. And he was a Navy SEAL.

Kai Aiona was a gorgeous man, who apparently was afraid of his sister, and had been so nice as to ask her on a date. And she had freaked.

With a sigh, she lifted the basket and carried it into the kitchen. She would have to take that step when she could, but she knew she wasn't ready.

But at least she still had some kind of sexual desires. Kai had proven that. She had always had a thing for Asian or Polynesian men. She knew he was Hawaiian, but May said their mother had been white, and there was a little Chinese somewhere in their bloodline. Damn. Whatever his genetic makeup, it was one hell of a tasty mix.

And if she was still Jocelyn the Queen, she would have jumped at the chance of a date with him and would have gladly jumped his bones. She could just imagine how those large hands would feel over her skin, or how that fast mouth of his would work magic on her...

Regretfully, she pushed those ideas out of her mind and set to getting the fruit stored. She needed her rest and there was no use in thinking about a man she would never have.

two

By mid-afternoon the next day, Kai was ready to crash. It had been a bitch of a morning, and now that there was a threat of a nasty storm, he had called it a day and brought in the ships. In the tourist and fishing business, it wouldn't be wise to even mess with it. One screw-up, one injured or stranded tourist, and your company was gone. The storm clouds were already rolling in, and for the first time in months it looked like Honolulu was about to get hit with a pretty nasty storm.

He walked into Dupree's and found his sister manning the booth.

"Hey, bra, what's up?"

"Bad weather rolling in. I cancelled the afternoon outings."

She nodded. "I have a feeling we're going to either be so busy we won't get breaks or we're going to be dead. Not sure which one I'm wanting."

He smiled. "Since I did your little errand yesterday, I think I deserve a free lunch."

"Moocher." But it was said with an affection that he was used to with May. Less than two years apart in age, they had always been close and even more so after their mother had died when May was twelve and he fourteen. When most brothers and sisters were growing apart, their mother's death had brought them closer together. And while there were times he'd hated it in high school, he now counted himself lucky.

"How about a plate of Kalua pig?"

She nodded. "Come on. I'll take my break with you."

After she grabbed them both a plate, they settled in the back booth by the kitchen. "So, you had no problem getting in Cynthia's house?"

He shook his head and finished the bite. "No. Jocelyn was there."

She'd been raising her fork to her mouth but stopped and looked at him. "Jocelyn didn't have a problem with letting you in the house?"

"A little at first." He jerked his shoulder, trying to forget the way she had treated him. "But she seemed to feel a little better when I mentioned your name."

"Oh." She didn't resume eating.

He stopped and looked at her. When she didn't say anything else, he asked, "What?"

She sighed. "It's just that she has been through a bad time."

"Yeah, she told me."

"She told you about Greg? I'm not sure how much she told the boss."

He shrugged again. "So, she had a bad breakup."

"No. She wasn't dating the man. He was her boss at one time. I'm not sure what happened, but in the end, she was in the hospital."

That had him setting his fork down. "Really?"

She rolled her eyes. "Remember when I was in the hospital, after the whole crazy bitch Lee thing?"

Of course, he did. It was hard to forget the crazy woman who had tried to kill his sister. The other woman's jealousy had driven her over the edge. The fact that May treated it like it was a common event, really irritated Kai.

"Chris was in Atlanta, remember? He had to go back there for her. She was admitted for a lot of things, including exhaustion."

"She had a breakdown?" Which he couldn't see. She might have been uncomfortable with him the night before, but she didn't seem like the type to fall apart.

"No. She was attacked."

Anger churned his gut. "Attacked. By the guy?"

She nodded. "I'm not sure exactly what went on, but I'm still amazed she let you in."

He sighed then dug back into his food. "Well, shit. I wasn't sure what it was. It didn't make sense, but I thought it was because of being Hawaiian."

She rolled her eyes. "Really, can you imagine Chris having a sister who was prejudiced? No, she is just a little skittish around men. I thought for sure they would be out for dinner."

After swallowing a fork full of food, he said, "Oh, well, she seemed okay with it."

"Either way, just be sure to be nice to her."

He rolled his eyes. The woman would always think she could tell him what to do. "It isn't like I was an ass to her. And it isn't like we are going to spend a lot of time together."

"She's coming over tomorrow night for the cookout. Dad's making some huhi huhi chicken. I thought it would be easier for her to meet everyone that way."

His heart did a little jerk as his body warmed. Just the thought of seeing her again was getting a reaction out of him, which was not a good thing in his humble opinion. He'd been steering clear of women for a month or two now, for good reason. He definitely didn't need a woman with so much baggage.

"I was planning a poker night with the guys tomorrow night."

May paused in lifting the fork to her mouth again. She narrowed her eyes and pursed her lips. *Shit.*

"No, you don't. You are not missing my party."

Kai knew it was a lost argument, but he couldn't keep himself from doing it just the same. Old habits with siblings die hard. "It's not your party. It's at our house."

She sighed. "It isn't like I'm trying to fix you up. And if you want to, make sure to invite your crew."

Just thinking of his crew intermingling with the group caused his lips to twitch.

"I mean, if you want to avoid her, I'm sure one of them would be happy to spend time with her."

He stopped smiling.

"I thought you said she was recovering."

May rolled her eyes. "Yeah. But it doesn't mean she's dead. And your guys are nice."

He snorted. "Nice? Do you mean just the ones without records?"

She shook her head. "Kai, you know most of the charges stem from bar fights."

Sometimes May was a little too naïve, but he figured he'd let her think his men were just misunderstood. Otherwise, she would start worrying.

"I guess I can make it tomorrow night."

She smiled, bright, sunny, and dammit, she had done all of that on purpose. He'd known it from the beginning but couldn't seem to stop himself. She did it to him every chance she could get. From the time she could talk, May was clever with a devious bent.

"I'll probably be late."

She rolled her eyes. "That's fine. Just as long as you get your butt there."

He was walking to his truck when he realized just how well she played him. May knew that Jocelyn was his type, would be a woman he would take an interest in. His sister was a pain in the ass. Damn. He needed to stay far away from Jocelyn, and he knew May. She was going to try and pair them up.

Well, he would just avoid her as much as possible. It would be easy enough with that many people there. Knowing May, she'd invited a lot of people, maybe even some people from Rough 'n Ready, which made him frown. Jocelyn didn't strike him as a person who would be interested in that. Or, if she was, someone who had been attacked probably shouldn't be involved in anything to do with the life his sister and brother-in-law lived. He didn't disagree with it, other than he didn't like to think of his sister doing those types of things. That was just not right. But he knew without a doubt that it wasn't the thing for Jocelyn.

He groaned. Shit, he was coming up with reasons she couldn't be involved with someone from the BDSM club his brother-in-law co-owned with Micah Ross. Why? It wasn't as if anything would happen between them. He had sworn off damaged women and she didn't seem that interested in him.

But as he turned on Kapolani Boulevard, he knew he wasn't

being truthful with himself. There was just something about Jocelyn Dupree with the sad eyes.

JOCELYN SMILED as Mr. Aiona gave her a glass of water.

He returned the smile. "If I had known Chris had such a beautiful sister, I'd have made him bring you over here years ago."

This she could handle. May's father was a short, happy man. He flirted with her, but he was harmless. As was May's grandfather who asked her if she would be interested in a bingo date.

Before she could answer, Chris slung his arm over her shoulders. "What? You thought that someone in my family wouldn't be gorgeous? With me as her brother?"

"Ah, but you're ugly," Mr. Aiona said. "How would I have known such a beauty would be related you?"

Her brother laughed, the happy sound warming her heart. In the last few months, he had rarely laughed around her. It was one of the things that made her feel even guiltier for what had happened. She knew it wasn't her fault, but it didn't make it any easier to know that she had caused her family and friends worry.

She took a long drink then said, "I have it on good authority that out of everyone, Shannon and I got all the looks. The boys are just ugly as sin."

"How many brothers do you have?" Mr. Aiona asked.

"Three. Although Chris is the worst of the bunch. Being the oldest, he always thought he could boss us around."

Before Mr. Aiona could ask her another question, she heard the door behind her shut. Even without looking, she knew who it was. She glanced over her shoulder, and though she had tried to prepare herself, she couldn't stop her body's reaction to him.

Kai Aiona had been gorgeous a few days ago, but tonight, damn, he was mouth-wateringly delicious. He was wearing a Hawaii University T-shirt that stretched over his massive chest, leaving little to her imagination. He was built, that was for sure, his shorts were short and stopped just above his knees. It gave her an excellent view of a dragon tattoo on his right leg.

She let her gaze travel back up his body. His hair was wet, as if he just stepped out of the shower which means he had been naked just a few minutes ago.

For the first time in months, she felt a jolt of awareness and need. It left her a little dizzy and her entire body warm.

"Kai. You're late." It wasn't said as an accusation but said by his father with a smile and a wealth of affection.

"Sorry, Dad. I picked up some more ice because I figured you'd be running low. Then I had to rinse the fish smell off me."

He gave his father a hug and then turned to face her.

Mr. Aiona's smile took on a conspiratorial slant. "Jocelyn, this is my son, Kai. He's my oldest."

"We met the other night," she said, without taking her gaze from Kai.

"You did?" This came both from Mr. Aiona and her brother.

She laughed, then looked at Mr. Aiona. "Yeah. He stopped by my first night with a basket from May. And I sent him home with sugar cookies."

Kai smiled and it brought out two dimples. Lord.

"They were delicious, thank you."

"Cookies? I never had any cookies." His father sounded suspicious.

She looked at Mr. Aiona, then to Kai. "I sent a dozen home with Kai."

A blush stained Kai's cheeks. Oh, wow. That was kind of cute and sexy in a totally weird way. "I ate them on the way home."

"All twelve?" she asked.

His father let out a booming laugh and slapped Kai on the back. "You'll get fat, my son."

"Not a chance. I'm going to grab a beer. Does anyone want anything?"

No one did and she watched him walk away. Inwardly, she sighed. It had been a long time since a man had caught her attention, but it seemed her libido had just come back to life. Damn, the man was put together fine. As she had noticed the night she met him, he wasn't tall, but he was built. She studied the way the worn fabric moved over his shoulders and could tell that he was definitely defined. And from what Cynthia said, he had more than just that dragon tattoo.

She noticed that her brother and Mr. Aiona had gotten quiet. Kai's father wore a knowing smile that had her face heating in embarrassment. God, how horrible. Caught ogling his son. When she turned to Chris, his thunderous expression didn't settler her nerves. She didn't need her brother going into protection mode the first night she met all of his friends.

Jocelyn knew she needed to get out of there. Chris was opening his mouth to say something when Cynthia walked up and saved Jocelyn from his wrath. She slipped her arm through Jocelyn's and tugged.

"May, Dee, and I want some girl time with Jocelyn. Go look at the meat and make manly sounds."

Chris didn't look all that happy about it, but he wasn't about to make a scene, especially with Cynthia pulling her away.

Once they were out of earshot, she said, "Girl, thank you. That was embarrassing."

Cynthia laughed. "Yeah, I could see that. I can't blame you. Kai is hot. And he is a sweetie."

Again, Jocelyn felt her face heat. "Yeah, well, nothing like lusting after a man in front of my brother. Not to mention his father. I thought Chris was going to say something."

Cynthia's blue eyes sparkled with mischief. "I'm sure he wanted to, but he has to weigh how it will look. If he makes too big of a scene, he's afraid Kai will intrigue you even more."

Jocelyn stopped and pulled her arm out of Cynthia's. "What does he think I am, fifteen?"

"Yeah, I think so. He still sees you that way. And I'm going to warn you, Chris is going to be overprotective."

She laughed. "Yeah, tell me something I don't know. He's always been that way. My first date he sat on the couch pretending to clean our daddy's gun."

"No, really?"

Jocelyn sighed. "Yeah. First real date and he wouldn't hold my hand. He acted like I had some kind of disease. Chris can be a pain in the ass."

"Of course." Cynthia slipped her arm through Jocelyn's again. "I just want you to know that he was so very scared when we went to Atlanta."

Shame washed through her. She should have never allowed it, should have never been in that position. Greg had pretty much escalated things and it had been out of her control in the end. But it didn't mean that every day she didn't fight the battle of shame versus anger. She'd learned through therapy she had to quit blaming herself, but there was a part of her that never would. It was the part that hated her family had been hurt by Greg's actions and the resulting incident.

"Don't start looking like that," Cynthia said.

She glanced at her soon-to-be sister-in-law. The militant expression on her soft features almost made Jocelyn smile. She might be petite, but Cynthia could be a tiger when it came to people she cared about.

"I hate that he went through that," Jocelyn said.

"I don't want you to feel guilty. You have no reason to be. It was bad, worse than I am sure you told us."

Jocelyn looked away because it was the truth. And she could feel the press of hot tears against the backs of her eyes.

"Hey, stop. If you cry, I'll cry."

She fought back the tears and looked at Cynthia who was wearing one of the most devious smiles she'd ever seen.

"What?"

"I just want you to understand and not kill him." She hesitated, then continued. "I would hate to raise our child alone."

For a second, what Cynthia said didn't sink in. When it did, Jocelyn opened her mouth, but Cynthia shook her head. "I haven't told him. I just found out today and I had to tell someone. If I had said something to him, he would have freaked out. And I didn't want the party to be about that."

"Cynthia, oh, God, I'm so happy for you." The first Dupree child of the next generation. Giddiness filled Jocelyn.

She smiled. "I am pretty happy too. We weren't really trying, but since Anna and Max—you know Max, Chris's best friend, had their first three months ago, I started having the pangs."

"You haven't told anyone else?"

She shook her head and stopped to look at Jocelyn. "I wanted to tell family first, and since you're my sister, I thought it would be nice. I'll tell Chris tonight after the party."

"I'm going to be an auntie."

Cynthia laughed. "You sure are. Now come on and meet Dee."

KAI WATCHED as Jocelyn and the other women stood around talking. She as wearing a jade green wrap dress. It hugged her slight curves and looked stunning against her brown skin.

He was trying not to pay attention to her, but he couldn't seem to keep himself from looking at her. It was understandable. The night he had met her he had been intrigued by her big doe eyes and that curvy body. Now though, she'd had rest and adjusted to island time, and she was nothing short of stunning. It was going to take more control than he thought he had to keep his hands off her. He would have to. There was no doubt about that. She might look like she had everything together, but now that he knew her background, he could see the signs. She rarely let men touch her, unless it was her brother. She'd shake hands when offered, but she kept the contact brief.

He turned to check the cooler to make sure they had enough drinks and almost ran into Chris. He was trying to look like he had casually walked up behind Kai, as if he had not a care in the world. But Kai read the intent in his eyes.

Shit.

"Hey, Kai."

He knew that tone, had heard it come out of his mouth many a time when dealing with men who were interested in his sister. "Hey."

"What are you doing?" Chris asked casually. Too casually.

"I was going to check the cooler to make sure we had enough to drink. Then I was going to go in and grab the rainbow salad."

Chris frowned. He was an easygoing guy, and it was one of the things that Kai liked about him. From the time he had hired May, Kai had felt comfortable with Chris. That was until tonight.

"I was sort of surprised Jocelyn didn't say anything yesterday about meeting you."

Kai shrugged. "Maybe I didn't make an impression on her."

Chris said nothing for a moment or two, but one eyebrow rose as he studied Kai. "Oh, I have a feeling it's the other way around."

Kai rolled his eyes. "Look, Chris, say what you came over here to say. I have things I gotta get done. If May's cookout isn't perfect, you know how mean she can get."

His lips twitched. May's boss knew well and good that you didn't mess with May's plans. "I just wanted you to know I really like you, but my sister...she isn't..."

"May said she had some trouble. Don't worry. While I think your sister is stunning, I promise hands off."

Again, Chris studied Kai and he had to fight the urge to fidget. But after a few moments, Chris's shoulders relaxed and he grinned. "Thanks. Normally, I wouldn't mind, but she's had a hard time. She is just getting back on track."

"No problem."

"With everything that happened, she lost her boyfriend and most of her working relationships. It was really hard on her."

Kai shook his head. "Believe me, I know what it's like to be in a bad relationship."

A knowing look came into Chris's eyes and Kai needed to escape.

"I better get that rainbow salad."

Chris said nothing but nodded as Kai turned to walk back into the house. Kai hated that everyone knew about Keisha and what she had done to him. He had always been private about the women he dated, but when they had gotten serious, everyone had figured it out. Keisha had worked at Rough 'n Ready as a waitress while they were dating. The whole sad thing played had out in front of his family.

The one thing he couldn't deal with was the careful handling. He hated it, but he used it at the same time. He avoided questions and people assumed it was because he was still hurting.

He'd just taken the first swig of beer when his brother-in-law sauntered into the kitchen. He would have never picked a man like Evan for his sister. Hell, he didn't want to think about the way their relationship had started at Evan's BDSM club, but Kai knew without a doubt, Evan was dedicated to May.

"You're a brave man, Evan."

He smiled and spread his hands wide. "What do you mean?"

Kai tsked. "Late to a party that May is throwing. I wouldn't want to be you, bra."

He laughed. "Ah, but she loves me more than she loves you.

And you shouldn't be talking. I take it you're in here to do her bidding."

He nodded. "After being grilled by Chris about his sister, I thought it wise to disappear for a while."

Evan's demeanor changed in a flash. The easygoing smile dissolved into a frown, and he narrowed his eyes. Crossing his arms over his chest, he asked, "You hit on Jocelyn?"

Kai should have realized that Evan would see Jocelyn as a little sister. And now he had to contend with another inquisition. "Back off, bra. I was only admiring."

Evan studied him for a moment and then nodded. "Okay. Well, just be careful there."

Irritated, he took another swig of beer. "Christ, Chambers, let it go."

Something passed in Evan's eyes and then an understanding bloomed there. "Sorry. I thought you might be ready to start dating again."

Jesus, he would never be able to live his relationship with Keisha down. Taking May's worried pampering was bad enough, but having one of the guys act like that was beyond embarrassing. His tough-guy status had been demolished by one little messed-up woman.

Thankfully, his sister had good timing for once. "What the hell is going on in here? I thought you were getting the salad, but you seem to have taken up residence in the kitchen. And you," she said pointing at Evan. "You're late."

Evan's demeanor softened as he looked at May. If Kai had ever had any kind of reservations about their relationship, they would be blown out to sea by just that look. It said only one thing to him. Complete and utter devotion.

"Ah, but you love me," Evan said as he walked toward her.

"Not that much," she said, but there was little heat in her words.

Evan pulled her into his arms and gave her a loud smacking kiss on the lips. "Forgive me, darlin'."

She sighed. "I guess I have to because I'm stuck with you. At least you arrived clean."

He smiled. "As promised. What do you need me to do?"

"Go watch Grandpa. He's already had too many beers and I have a feeling Micah might beat him over the head if he hits on Dee anymore."

He gave her another kiss, then slipped out the door.

"You having any problems with Chris?"

Kai shook his head as he opened the drawer and retrieved a spoon for the salad. "Just a jackass brother trying to warn me off his sister." He smiled at her. "Been in his shoes before."

She frowned at him, and he could almost hear her brain working it through. "Who?"

He sighed. "Tommy Dixon."

She made a face. "He was your best friend."

"Was being the operative word. You don't try and sleep with your best friend's sister."

She sighed. "He didn't get anywhere. He tried to kiss me and I smacked him upside the head."

"Doesn't matter. There's a code."

She rolled her eyes. "Brothers are stupid."

"You can say that again." Jocelyn's amused voice, laced with that thick New Orleans' accent, filtered into the kitchen.

He looked over at her. A small smile played over her full, sensual lips and he found himself mesmerized by her unpainted mouth. The woman wore little makeup, and he found that he liked that. Her natural beauty was more than enough for him.

"I swear, I'm lucky I'm so smart or their stupidity would have rubbed off on me," May said with a smile. "Having issues with the boss?"

Jocelyn rolled her eyes. "Always. I was wondering if you need any help."

May shook her head and walked toward her and slipped her arm over Jocelyn's shoulders. It was funny looking because May was so much shorter than Jocelyn.

"One thing about brothers, since they're so stupid, they tend to do what I tell them. Kai's getting the rainbow salad. I want to get you in a corner and learn embarrassing things about Chris from his childhood. That way, I'll have some leverage at work."

Jocelyn laughed and the sound of it wrapped around him. Not a tinkle, but full bodied, seductive and downright arousing. He watched them walk out of the kitchen and his gaze roamed down Jocelyn's back, to the fine ass. She was wearing jeans today and it did little to hide her curvy backside.

"Kai?" May asked.

He shook his head and pulled his attention away from Jocelyn's ass.

"Coming."

He just needed to remind himself she was off-limits. She didn't need a man bothering her and he definitely didn't need another heartbreak. The last one was enough to last him a lifetime.

three

"I'm glad you liked the cookies."

The moment he heard her voice, his body reacted. It was hard not to. Kai smiled as he turned to face Jocelyn. "Not surprising since you graduated at the top of your class."

She rolled her eyes. "How did you know that?"

He chuckled. "Chris. He brags a lot about you."

Her smile faded and something he couldn't discern moved over her face. "Yeah, well, I just wanted to be sure that you didn't think I was rude the other night."

"No problem."

She fidgeted with the water bottle that she was drinking from and the silence between them stretched. It was uncomfortable and odd considering she had come looking for him. He glanced over her shoulder and noticed she had waited until her brother was busy.

"Chris didn't say anything rude to you, did he?"

He shook his head. "Not really."

Her lips twitched and her eyes sparkled. "I apologize. It's just that he noticed..."

She trailed off, her face brightened, and she looked away.

Knowing that she was embarrassed, and liking the stain of color on her cheeks, he had to poke fun. "What?"

She swallowed and looked back at him. "Nothing. Chris has always been kind of overprotective, and now he's a little worse."

He nodded. "Being an older brother, I can understand."

"May doesn't seem like the kind of woman who would put up with interference. And since you're afraid of her—"

"What makes you think that?"

"You drove all the way to the windward side of the island to give me a basket on a Saturday night. I mean...I have been hearing about your escapades for years from May. Lord knows you probably had something to do."

Damn his sister. Knowing her, she made him sound like some kind of Don Juan of Oahu. He dated around, that was true, but it still irritated him that his sister acted as if he slept with any available woman.

"Well, don't believe everything you hear."

She laughed. God, she was beautiful when she laughed. It brightened her face and her eyes sparkled. He loved a woman who laughed with her whole body. "Most of it was good. She told me you're a good guy. And she told me you do some sight-seeing tours."

He nodded and took a sip from his beer bottle. "I have several boats. One is just a fishing boat. I do a little commercial fishing. Mainly sell to your brother."

"And you do those deep-water fishing things."

"Yeah. I mostly handle the sightseeing tours."

"Good. I wanted to go, but I wanted to go with someone I know, and since I just got here..." She shrugged.

"Sure. Come on down tomorrow if you want. Tuesdays are slow sometimes. I know we have a few more spots open."

"Thanks." She walked away and he watched her, trying his best to ignore the way his blood danced every time he heard her laugh.

JOCELYN SMILED when she peeked through the window of Cynthia's Bakery. The place was packed, filled with customers on their way to work. She reached the door, but before she could open it Chris was there pushing it open.

He smiled at her. "Hey, you're up early."

Jocelyn shook her head. "You forget I'm still on Atlanta time."

He laughed and pulled her into the crowd, guiding her back behind the counter. It was a plain store with a glass counter accented in soft pink colors. Several small tables were scattered in the small space between the counter and the front door, all filled with customers. The only flourish in the design of the bakery was Cynthia's name plastered on everything—from the window front to the bags—in pink script. The scents of the bakery surrounded her, comforted her. Vanilla, chocolate, flour and sugar. It was a mix of aromas she knew well and missed.

"Morning, Jocelyn." Cynthia looked pale and a bit over-worked. Her blonde hair curled around her face, but Jocelyn could tell she was enjoying herself. The smile she offered each customer showed that she loved what she was doing. "Still not used to the Hawaiian time?"

"No. I think it might take a while after such a long move."

Cynthia nodded, and Jocelyn opened her mouth to ask if she needed help, but Cynthia was already turning away to chat with a customer.

"Come on back," Chris said as he guided her back to the office. He let her step away as he shut the door then leaned back against it.

She felt him studying her so she turned and smiled at him. "What?"

"When were you going to tell me?"

She frowned. "What do you mean?"

"Cynthia told me last night about the baby. And then she told me you knew."

She laughed. "Sorry, I was sworn to secrecy." She stepped closer and slipped her arms around him for a quick hug and kiss. "Daddy."

When she looked up, an expression of panic passed over his face.

"Aren't you happy?"

"Yeah, uh," he said, backing away from her. "Just a little nervous. And she's been kind of sick."

Jocelyn nodded. "I thought she looked a little pale."

"I hope this is the last morning. I can't take another wake-up call like that."

Jocelyn remembered Chris's gag reflex and the fact he couldn't stand the sound of retching. She dissolved into giggles. "Oh, God, you're getting morning sickness too."

"Shut up." But the smile he gave softened the rebuke. "What are you doing here anyway?"

"I can't seem to sleep past four in the morning."

He nodded. "It takes about three or four months to completely get over the time difference. Or it did for me."

"And I think I might take a boat ride today."

His eyes narrowed. "Anyone in particular you're going to go with?"

She sighed. "Get off it, Chris. I'm not going to get involved right now, and if I was it isn't any of your business. But I trust Kai to be responsible. From the online reviews, his sightseeing tours are considered some of the best on the island. I just thought I would do something touristy before I started looking for a job."

"I don't think you need to do that," Cynthia said.

Jocelyn smiled as she turned around and saw Cynthia there. "Hey, who's manning the front?"

"Hilary. She's my part-time help."

"I need full-time work."

"You don't need to work," Chris said.

She shared a look with Cynthia. "Yes, I do. I need to feel like I'm doing something. The last few months have been hard on me. I need to keep busy."

Chris opened his mouth to argue, but Cynthia came to her rescue. "I was talking full time. Or you can do some contracted work for me. I've been getting requests for cakes, which I can do, but not the big fancy things. Weddings especially. Hawaii has a lot of people who come here to marry but I don't have the skill. If you think you might want to do something like that, let me know." She walked around the table and kissed Chris on his forehead. "Feeling better, babe?"

"Fine," he grumbled.

"Just keep eating the crackers, it helps."

Jocelyn started giggling before her soon-to-be sister-in-law made it out the door.

"Shut up," he said, but there was little heat in it.

"Sorry, Daddy."

He smiled. "Mom is going to flip."

"First grandchild, you bet." She glanced at the time. "I better get going. I have an early tour."

His smiled dissolved. "Maybe I can make it out there with you today."

"Really? I mean, with the waves rocking the boat, well, that might not be good for the stomach of yours. The back and forth...up and down...and that salty, fishy air. Seems like it might be bad for you."

He swallowed. "That's not funny."

She giggled as she fell into the chair. "It seems pretty funny to me."

"I just thought you might want someone to show you around."

"That will be nice," she said. "But I am in the mood for a boat ride today. And I really don't want to play nursemaid to you."

"I should have let Malachai sell you when Mom brought you home from the hospital."

She laughed. "I missed you."

"You sure you're doing okay?"

She nodded. "Actually, I'm doing just fine. And—" she looked at the clock behind Chris's head, "—I better get going. I want to walk to the boat. It's just too beautiful not to."

JOCELYN ENJOYED the hum of Honolulu. She didn't think she could ever live in the city. She was a solitary soul, but she did like to get out and experience people. She loved watching their interactions, watching the activities. It made her feel alive. And right now, everything that had happened in the last year seemed so small, so inconsequential, that she sighed with happiness. She knew she had a long time before she would be completely healed. Truthfully, she knew she would never be the same person. The sexual harassment had taken a lot out of her. She had started hating work, hating her body, and dammit, he made her ashamed her of sexuality. Like she had brought it on herself.

Greg had known her insecurities. There were plenty, and being her mentor and friend, he had learned them all. And he had used them against her, chopping away at her confidence.

The last two months, the new job, the attack...she shoved the thoughts to the back of her mind. She couldn't deal with it now, wouldn't until she knew she could. Unmedicated. She stopped at a street corner waiting for the light to change. She'd gone three weeks without meds, and it had been tough, but she was just enjoying the act of experiencing life again. The medication they'd had her on had made her numb.

She walked across the street and to the tour boat area.

Brightly colored boats bobbed in the water as she walked down the plank. Jocelyn loved the sound of waves slapping against the wood as she meandered toward the slip where Kai's boat was. She had never really been a boat person. Not one who would spend all day out on a boat. Growing up in New Orleans, boats were a way of life. She had enough friends who had family out in the bayou or family who worked in the Gulf. It had just never been something that called to her. Still, the idea of just enjoying the crystal blue waters and beautiful scenery appealed to her. Especially today. She was feeling a little restless in Cynthia's little house, and if she hadn't gotten out she would have been baking up a storm. Being without anything to do, she would end up eating the majority of them. Her ass could not take that.

She walked past one last boat and found Kai's. It was white with blue trim, and it looked empty at first glance. Then Kai walked to the front of the boat, and she lost most rational thought. He was shirtless. God almighty, he was gorgeous. He wasn't steroid big. No, this was the kind of muscle that came from good, honest, physical work.

He bent over to grab some rope and she sighed. Even at this distance, she could see the ripple of muscle beneath the flesh. Damn. He was golden brown that came from his Hawaiian background, and his time spent out in the sun. Tattoos decorated his upper arms, and as he turned she saw one that stretched across his back. All of the designs had a Hawaiian feel to them. She could imagine tracing the design with her fingertip, enjoying the feel of his smooth skin beneath hers. Someone leaned over the railing from up above, one of his crew she presumed, and said something to Kai. He threw his head back and laughed. She could barely hear it, but it sent a shaft of need rushing through her blood. She stopped where she was and drew in a deep breath. It had been very long since she'd been interested, and now, she wanted. It was that same sexual rush she'd lost almost a year before, a year before when Greg had ruined it for her.

The same crewmember said something else, and Kai turned around and spotted her. The smile that curved his lips as she approached sank into her skin. Damn, could another man be as pretty as Kai Aiona? Deeply bronzed skin, green eyes, and a body of an Adonis. He was going to be very hard to ignore.

She ordered herself to start moving forward and reminded

herself that she wasn't ready for a man. Especially not one like Kai Aiona.

KAI WATCHED Jocelyn walk down the plank. A few days rest had done the woman wonders. She needed a little more meat on those fabulous bones, he thought. She was definitely still attractive, but Kai liked curves on a woman.

"Morning, Jocelyn," he said, trying to ignore the way his heart was beating against his chest. He hadn't been this taken with a woman since he was sixteen.

"Good morning. I hope I'm not too early."

He shook his head and held his hand out to her. "No. I usually make other people wait, but since you're sort of family, you can come on for a quick tour."

The moment she placed her hand in his, he felt an electric spark rush through his body. Jocelyn shivered, so she felt it too. Each time he saw her, the attraction seemed to grow. That was usually a good thing, but this time it wasn't. He didn't need a woman with a damaged heart, not when he was trying to fix his. As he helped her down the steps, the heat of her drew him closer. Her rich, delicious scent surrounded him. The aroma of the docks was overpowering, but he didn't seem to notice the smell of salt and fish. Instead, he could only seem to sense vanilla and sugar.

His mouth dried up. Damn, he wanted one big bite.

He pulled in a deep breath as he turned and found his crew already in front of them, waiting to be introduced. He sighed.

"Jocelyn, this is Tommy," he said, motioning to his captain.

Tommy was about ten years older than Kai and looked at least three years younger. The blond haired, blue-eyed Texan still got carded when they went out. But that never seemed to hurt him, especially with their older customers. A lot of cougars had been booking trips together for sight-seeing tours, and they seemed to have a thing for Tommy.

He motioned to Vince, the oldest and probably meanest of the group. Twenty years in the merchant marines had toughened the old man, and he pretended to hate most women, especially when they were on the boat. But even he was smiling.

"This is Vince, and behind him—" he pointed to the tall, broad-shouldered Jamaican, "—is Paul."

"Hi," Jocelyn said.

"Oh, Lord, you didn't tell us we would have someone from New Orleans on the boat," Tommy said.

Her eyes widened. "You could tell that just form me saying hi?"

He nodded. "I grew up in Beaufort and spent a lot of time in New Orleans."

She laughed. "We'll have to get together and see if we know any of the same people. You know what they say."

Tommy's smile widened. "Everyone knows everyone else in New Orleans."

He stepped forward but came to an abrupt halt when Kai growled. His captain's eyes widened then he laughed.

Kai glanced at Jocelyn who was looking at him as if he had grown a second head. And why not? He was acting as if she were his territory. She didn't even know how out of character it was for him to behave that way. He ignored her and turned his attention back to his crew.

"Don't you men have something to do?"

Vince rolled his eyes, Paul winked at Jocelyn, making her blush, and Tommy smiled at Kai as they went back to work.

"Sorry about that."

She laughed again, the sound making his head spin. "No, I like them. Very...diverse."

"They are that. Come on, I'll show you around a little bit."

He gave her a tour, trying to concentrate on showing her all the little interesting things tourists liked to see. In the back of his mind though, were his worries about his reaction. He was attracted, yes. What man in his right mind wouldn't be? She was gloriously put together. Long limbs, smooth skin and a luscious body once she got her weight back. From what May said, Jocelyn had been much more rounded before her situation a few months ago. So, he knew with Chris and May around, the woman would definitely get back to her regular curves. "You said you do most of these tours?"

He nodded as he looked over the bow. "I'm the best at handling customers, although Tommy can be good. He gets a little more...involved with the single female passengers, though."

"Yeah, I can see that."

"Would you like a drink of something? Soda, water?"

"I'll take a water."

He went to retrieve it, his mind back on his reaction to her. Being attracted to her was normal, even expected, but Kai never felt territorial. Not even when he was dating someone. He had never been a man who wanted to fight over a woman. Well, until he had started dating Keisha again, then found out she didn't want to be that serious. Of course, he had played it off. She had come to him as a friend and lover. Why would she have expected more from him? He had a reputation and that was all Keisha had wanted. And he had fooled himself in thinking he could change her mind by giving her just what he had always given women. When she up and left the island to follow some man she just met, he'd realized that he wasn't cut out for it. He wouldn't make the mistake again. Mutual breakups were more his style.

"I say he's dating her."

Tommy's voice flitted over common area. Shit, he should have known they would be speculating about Jocelyn. She was just his type, and he did have a thing for African-American women. They all knew because they had seen him single out women who had more than one thing in common with Jocelyn. That sweet smile with a hint of wickedness would normally have him pushing for a serious date.

He saw Vince shake his head and open his mouth and Kai knew he had to stop the talk about it or it could get out of hand. Plus, Jocelyn might not like being discussed.

"I'd say you were wrong."

They all turned around and faced Kai, not one guilty look in the crowd. He was used to this, but he didn't like anyone talking about Jocelyn. Another oddity for him.

"She's Chris's sister, my sister's boss. She just moved here and knows no one."

Tommy's grin widened. "So, you're saying she's fair game."

He tossed a look at him and went to the cooler. "I say you might be out of a job if you push to date her."

The crew went quiet when he looked around. "What?"

"Nothing," Tommy said. "Nothing at all."

Irritated, he shoved them out of his mind as he climbed the stairs back up the deck. He saw her sitting there, the crisp white linen shirt, red capris and sandals had him gulping. It wasn't particularly sexy, but with her, it didn't seem to matter. He had seen her toes earlier and they were painted. Red. God, how was he supposed to ignore a woman with red toenails who had every physical requirement he desired in a woman? He would have to be a saint, and that was something he never aspired to.

She noticed him and smiled as he approached. He felt that little hitch in his heart again. *Damn.*

"Thanks. I'm used to heat, but it has been a while since I've lived near the water. The salt in the air can sometimes zap your moisture away."

He nodded and gulped down half his bottle. She sipped at hers as she watched him with those emerald mermaid eyes. Kai knew it was wrong, knew that it would cause all kinds of complications, but he wanted to see her, needed to. Not just today. Tomorrow, or the next day. Or both. Damn, this compulsion was going to drive him insane, and he hadn't even spent that much time with her. He gave in.

He took one last swallow of water. "Okay, I have to ask again."

"Yes?"

He opened his mouth, but the sound of the other travelers reached him, and he grimaced. His timing with women had been off for months, but it seemed to be worse around Jocelyn. She was watching him patiently waiting for his question.

"It'll have to wait. Want to meet the other passengers?"

She eyed him for a minute then nodded. "Sure."

JOCELYN WATCHED Kai talking to a small girl about four years old. He was good with people. In the last two hours, she'd found herself amazed at his patience. She had been in the public-services industry for years, but rarely had this much contact with the public. And for good reason. She couldn't take the constant attention they wanted. Or the whining, or well, them.

She chuckled to herself as she remembered her run in with a bridezilla two years ago. The girl had wanted to make changes the morning of her wedding to both the groom's cake and the official wedding cake. She'd had the nerve to threaten Jocelyn's job. It must have taken her a long time to get that icing out of her hair after Jocelyn had dropped it on the woman's head.

She settled back against the bench and looked out over the water. She had spent her childhood in New Orleans, and a ton of her time near the Gulf of Mexico and the Atlantic Ocean. Neither could compare to the crisp turquoise of the Pacific. It was smooth as glass today. She could see the coastline as they chugged along, and she drew in a deep breath. The air was so clean, so vibrant. She closed her eyes and enjoyed the warmth of the sun on her face.

"Enjoying yourself?"

She slowly opened her eyes and found Kai standing beside her. Without invitation, he slid into the seat to the right of her.

"Yeah, I am. I've always liked the water. It's one of the things I missed most when I lived in Atlanta."

He nodded. "I don't think I could live landlocked."

He looked out over the boat, and she could see him taking note of what was going on. He might play the easygoing guy, but she recognized a businessman when she saw him. He might have picked something that he loved, but in his heart, he understood his responsibilities. And dammit, that made him even more enticing.

"It's different though."

He turned his attention back to her face and she wished she could see what he was thinking. His sunglasses made it hard.

"Different?"

"Yeah. I was just thinking of the Gulf and how it's so different than this."

"Hmm. I'll have to take your word for it. I've never been there."

She cocked her head to the side. "Not many trips to the mainland?"

He shook his head. "I've been to the west coast, we have family there, and to Japan and China. But I get a little buggy when I'm on the mainland."

"I can't see you reacting that way anywhere. You seem so laid-back."

He shrugged. "Too many rules. Too many people."

She laughed and he stilled.

"What?" she asked when he continued to stare at her.

He swallowed convulsively. "I like your laugh."

There was a hint of heat threaded in the words that hadn't been there before. She ordered herself not to pay attention, to not let it get to her. It was hard because she knew without a doubt he would be good in bed. It was easy to see in the way he moved, all power and grace. Plus, he was patient, so a woman had to know that he would do everything in his power to make it worth her time.

She swallowed.

"Why did you laugh?" he asked.

"Oh, because someone living on Oahu saying there are too many people is kind of funny. This place is crowded."

He leaned back and looked out over the water, then back at

her. "There are a lot of places you can find solitude. LA, hard to find. And too much pollution." He shook his head in disgust.

"That's one of the things I hated about Atlanta. The pollution was starting to get to me. I have to say I do like the Windward side of the island better. It seems to be at a slower pace."

He nodded. "I like it. There are other places...if you would like a tour guide?"

She studied him, still irritated that she couldn't see his eyes. Without seeing them she didn't know what his expression was. And she knew from the tone it wasn't just a friendly invite. Kai saw it as a date. He didn't ever attempt to couch it any other way and she liked him even better for it. A devious man would pretend to want to be only friends and try to talk her into bed. Kai wouldn't do that. He didn't need to.

God help her, she wanted to try. She wanted to go out with a man who wanted to spend time with her and wasn't psychoanalyzing her every move. It would be fun to just be Jocelyn and enjoy her day out. Like today.

"I'd like that."

He seemed to relax at her agreement. Had he been worried she would say no? Why? From the looks of the other female passengers, he could easily find a hook-up tonight. Or any night for that matter. Just the fact he was worried she would say no interested her.

"Tell you what, before you leave let me have your phone number. I'll give you a call and take you on a tour. Nothing like seeing the island with a *Kama'aina.*"

She waited for the instinctive freak out. In the last few months, any time a man made any kind of overture she had freaked out. An unknown man holding the door open for her would have her backing away from him. But with Kai, it wasn't there. The only feeling she had was the rush of excitement over going on a date. Just for that alone she wanted to kiss him. Beyond that, she wanted to get to know him better.

"Sure."

"Gotta get back to work."

She watched him walk back to the helm, chatting with the tourists as he went. She slipped her gaze down his back to his fine ass and amazing legs. She also noticed a few of the other women noticing, and she tried to squash the jealousy that surged. She had no business being jealous. Flirting was fine, almost mandatory to her recovery. But she knew she wasn't ready for anything more than that.

Even if her body was throbbing and begging her to be bad. She wasn't ready, only a month from being the zombie her drugs had made her. No. A nice uncomplicated day with Kai exploring the island would be fun, and that was all.

He turned to start talking to the crowd. But in one instant, he looked at her, and even without seeing his eyes she knew he had zeroed in on her. He gave her a slow, sexy smile she felt all the way to the tips of her toes.

For the first time in a long time, she realized she looked forward to time alone with a very attractive man.

She leaned back again and closed her eyes. This had been a banner day.

four

Three days later, Jocelyn stopped cold when she saw the crowd that was gathered in the diner. She knew when her brother had invited her, but maybe he hadn't expected Kai Aiona there. From the muttered curse behind her, she figured not. She tossed him a look over her shoulder and saw the frown he was trying to hide.

She tried to ignore it and gave the table a smile. Dee and Micah were there, along with May and Evan. There were two chairs on one side, and an empty one beside Kai.

"I didn't know if we would see y'all tonight," Evan said as they approached.

"I had a nap this afternoon, and now I'm famished," Cynthia said.

That much was true. While Chris had been at work, Jocelyn had stopped by their house for some baby talk. Being the one sibling who lived on the island with Chris, Jocelyn was taking her duties as auntie very seriously. Within thirty minutes, Cynthia had been falling asleep. The four-hour nap had left her soon-to-be sister-in-law alert and hungry. Which sort of amazed

Jocelyn knowing how bad her morning sickness had been. Chris, being the way he was, couldn't say no to Cynthia when Evan had called them up.

"Plus, I wanted to see the best place to eat in Honolulu at closing time," Jocelyn said.

Micah laughed. "It is that. Not great for the cholesterol, but damned fine food." She eyed the club owner. He was the tallest of all the men at the table, with long, straight black hair, and there was no denying he was Native American. The man didn't seem to have an ounce of fat on his body.

She inched around the table, making her way to the empty seat beside Kai. He stood as she approached. It shouldn't have made her heart go pitter patter, but it was hard for her to ignore her upbringing. She was her own woman, but she'd been raised on Southern manners. When a guy held doors or stood when she approached, it got to her.

"So, I take it we're the fifth wheels?'

He laughed. "Of course. But then, they're stuck with the same person forever. We have variety."

"Yeah, you got that right." She looked around the diner that was in the heart of Honolulu. The red booths were worn but clean, and the bright overhead lighting, along with the soda-shop counter and outfits worn by the staff, reminded her of Al's from Happy Days. "I haven't been here yet."

He shook his head. "Best place to eat in the area. *Onoliscious*," he said, using the word Hawaiians used to describe the most delicious food. "Of course, diners usually are."

The waiter came up asking for her drink order and asked if they had decided on food.

"Have the burger. It's one of the best, greasiest things around."

She smiled at the waiter. "I'll have a cheeseburger."

He wrote it down, collected her menu and moved down the line.

"So, is this the drunk gathering?"

He nodded. "I haven't been here in a while, but we used to come later at night."

As if to prove his point, a burst of laughter filled the diner as a group of twenty-somethings—if that—crowded the lobby area.

"Are you getting settled in?" he asked, leaning closer.

She nodded. "I think I'll be taking you up on that tour. I don't want to do the touristy thing anymore. I'm ready to learn where the locals go."

He smiled and her heart turned over. Kai was laid-back so a smile was normal to see on him, but he had different smiles. Some were innocent, but this one was lethal to her libido. It warmed his eyes as he leaned closer. "Tomorrow should be a good day. Weather's gonna be nice."

She laughed. "The weather is always nice. It's Hawaii."

"Right. But the wind will be light which will make for an easier sightseeing tour."

"So, Jocelyn, what are you planning on doing?"

The abrupt question came from May, and she thought she heard Micah laugh. Subtly apparently wasn't something May was good at. She took her time to look away from Kai and face the long table of couples.

"Cynthia's taking pity on me and hiring me."

"Oh, please. Girl is considered one of the top pastry chefs in the country and she's going to be at *Cynthia's*." The bright light of success lit Cynthia's blue eyes. "I'm going to make some big money."

Jocelyn felt her cheeks burn. It used to be a source of a pride to be considered a top pastry chef. Heck, if she could have, she would have announced it everywhere. But now, it was a sort of embarrassment. Not for her accomplishments, those she was proud of. Now though, she had fallen so far and had barely made it through the last few months.

"I'm just taking it day by day."

"And she's not starting work until next week," her brother announced.

She smiled down the table at Chris even as annoyance inched down her spine. Good Lord, he was doing it again. She knew he had to be protective, but dammit, she was sick of being treated as if she couldn't handle herself. "Of course, there is always a chance Cynthia might have her hands full because of a mitigating circumstance."

With one look, she let her brother know she would let everyone know about his little morning sickness. She knew for a fact that Micah and Evan would never let him hear the end of it. Before he could say anything else, the waiter came with their drinks. With the reprieve, she turned her attention back to Kai. When she turned to him, he was studying her.

"I think tomorrow would be great for the tour."

He glanced at her brother then back to her. "Are you sure Chris doesn't mind?"

She shook her head. "I'm almost thirty. I can take care of myself. Besides, I didn't take you for such a wuss that a few dirty looks from my brother would bother you."

He took a sip of his soda as he continued to study her. "So, what about ten in the morning?"

She smiled. "You got it."

KAI WAS WALKING to his car when he heard the sound of feet behind him. He tensed, but he calmed down when he saw Chris's reflection in the store window to his right. He stopped and faced him. Kai had known this was coming.

"What do you think you're doing with my sister?" Chris asked. One thing about his sister's boss, he never beat around the bush. It was one of the things Kai had liked about Chris until recently. And it shouldn't have hurt, but it did, more than it did the other day. Chris must have sensed it.

Chris made a disgusted sound. "I told you it isn't that."

Kai waved it away and tried to push the feelings down. He should be used to it. There were still people who saw him as less. One because of his Hawaiian blood and two because he never made it to college. Hell, he didn't make it out of high school.

"I offered to take her around the island when she went on the boat tour. She said you haven't showed her around, and I thought she was kind of lonely."

Chris crossed his arms over his massive chest. He was taller than Kai and probably outweighed him. Still, both men knew that in a fair fight, Kai would probably kick his ass. Even knowing that, Chris looked ready to take him on. As an older brother, Kai had to give him some respect for that.

"And you were there ready to step in to help her with the loneliness."

Shit. He shouldn't be so pissed, because the truth was, he had a lot of relationships like that. He was known for it. He kept everything light, dated tourists or women looking for no more than a little fun. If he did more than that it caused problems.

"It isn't like that. Listen, she feels left out. And a little lost. I thought if I helped her get to know the island, she might venture out on her own."

Chris sighed, his shoulders slumping. "I have been so busy with Cynthia. Dammit, I should have thought of it."

"Listen, don't beat yourself up about it. Sisters aren't always forthcoming with their feelings."

"Yeah, I know, but I convinced her to move here then dumped her on the other side of the island."

"Believe me, if your sister was pissed, I have a feeling you'd know. She just wanted to get to know the island, and since I know it like the back of my hand, I figured it wouldn't hurt for her to see some of those places that aren't on the touristy maps."

Chris nodded. "I appreciate it. But like I said, she can't handle a relationship right now, and I will be damned if anyone will push her."

"Take it easy. Seriously, I do not have to coerce wounded women."

"Did May tell you what happened?"

He shook his head. "I don't want to know unless Jocelyn wants to tell me. I'm just trying to be friendly."

Chris didn't look like he believed him, and of course, he shouldn't. When she had been on his boat, knowing his reaction to her, he'd decided there was no use fighting it. He had wanted her from the moment she'd opened the door that first night. She might say no, and seriously, that was fine by him. He would never try and push her. But since she had been the first woman who had intrigued him like this in a few months, he knew better than to ignore it.

"I better get back to Cynthia before she gets even more pissed about me interfering."

"No problem."

He watched his sister's boss jog over to his car and Cynthia. The last few months had been hard since Keisha left, and every time he had been in the company of the group, he had felt left out. He never brought dates, not since Keisha had ripped his heart out and left the island. He rarely had before Keisha, truth be told. May had never been one for inviting him until he had started living like a monk. It was as if she pitied him, which he hated. He hated it even more that he didn't seem to be able to say no. Even surrounded by all the happy couples hadn't been as bad as being by himself.

He sighed and continued to walk to his car. A year ago, it wouldn't have bothered him, but now it did. It didn't mean he wanted a serious relationship. He had proven he wasn't made for them. But the feeling that he was being left out, somehow pitied by people had gnawed at him. But with Jocelyn there tonight it had been pretty bearable.

He unlocked his car and slid into the seat. She was even more gorgeous now. She had adjusted to the time difference. Only a dead man could ignore that infectious laugh. He could tell she did it a lot. The sound of joy that filled the diner when she laughed had left him mesmerized. Even sitting here over an hour later, he could remember the men who had turned in her direction when she laughed. And just how much he had wanted to kick their asses.

Damn, he needed to remember his role here. He was to be a friend with possible benefits. It was something he'd had no trouble with before Keisha, and he was happy to fill that role again. But as he drove off, he wondered what Jocelyn would be wearing tomorrow and just how many times he could get her to laugh.

KAI TURNED into Jocelyn's driveway and frowned. He knew the car parked there and knew he wasn't in the mood to go another round with Chris. Being the oldest and a brother, he understood wanting to protect your younger sister. It was hard to let her lead her own life. He knew that whatever had left the shadows in Jocelyn's beautiful eyes was pretty bad. But there was a point when a brother had to step back.

He drew in a deep breath as he got out of the car and headed to the porch. He knew this wasn't going to be fun. Chris knew Kai's reputation with women. It was all he could do not to kiss her. So, being the masochist that he was, he decided to take her out on a date. As he stepped on the lowest stair to the porch, he heard Jocelyn's sweet, sexy, New Orleans' voice drift out the open window.

"I didn't exactly ask your opinion."

"Jocelyn, you seem to be doing much better, but I don't understand this compulsion to go out with Kai."

For a few moments she said nothing. From his own experience, he knew that wasn't a good sign for Chris. "You don't think I would be attracted to him?"

"I didn't say that. But I thought you'd sworn off men."

"Obviously not all men because here you are," she said. He could hear the irritation rising in her voice and part of him wanted to leave. He didn't need any kind of big family drama. He'd had enough of that with Keisha a few months ago.

"I don't understand why I can't show you around."

"First, I don't want you to go all pukey on me while we are out."

"I am not pukey."

She ignored his comment and rolled right on. "And I want to go out with someone who isn't always watching me waiting for me to fall apart."

She had lowered her voice, and he could hear the deep pain beneath the surface of the words. But there was something else there. Determination. It was quietly infused in her voice, telling Kai that no matter how put together she seemed now, she was fighting her demons every day. That kind of inner strength was just too much to resist.

It had him walking up on the porch with as much noise as his slippers would provide and knocking on the door.

Jocelyn opened the door with a smile. "Hey, Kai. Come on in. I'm almost ready. In fact, I would have been if Chris hadn't bothered me this morning."

The smile she shot him was overly bright, but he didn't let it bother him. He had to contend with the brother who was right now giving him the stink eye.

"You said we are just going to drive around the island?"

He nodded. "You might want to make sure you wear slippas so that walking on the beach is easy."

She frowned and he heard Chris chuckle.

"Flip-flops, Jocelyn."

She glanced back over her shoulder at her brother, then turned, her smile now genuine. It reached her eyes, and he felt the slow thrum of lust beat through his blood.

"I'll be right back."

She turned and walked to the back of the small house. It took every bit of his power not to watch that full, round ass sway, but he did it. He turned his attention to her brother.

"Morning, Chris."

Chris stood there, his frown dark, his arms crossed over his massive chest. Kai wasn't afraid of him. He might be a bit bigger, but as May liked to point out, Kai spent a lot of his time on the docks. "Morning. You want to tell me what this is about?"

"I thought we went over that last night."

Chris shifted his feet. "I've been thinking about it, and I'm still not sure this is a good idea."

Kai held up his hands. "Give it a rest, bra. Your sister mentioned that she thought Oahu was crowded, I said I would show her some of the other spots that weren't."

"You aren't making any moves on her."

Not a question, a statement with a threat attached by way of his tone. Kai knew his life would be easier to deny it completely, but Chris was too smart. It wasn't in Kai's ability to lie, not when he was this attracted to a woman.

"Your sister is an attractive woman who is discovering Hawaii. What goes on between us is just that. Between us."

Chris said nothing.

"Look at it this way, man. You want me to take her around, or some other man? Your sister is gorgeous and bright. Men are attracted to her because of her looks, but I am sure they stick around because of the personality. You know you can trust me."

For a second, he was sure that Chris was going to argue with him, but then his shoulders relaxed.

"Sorry. I really am. All of us have been a bit overprotective since her hospital stay. I know I can trust you, it's just..."

Kai smiled. "She's your sister. I understand. Listen, I've been in your shoes. May always attracted a lot of men."

He nodded and opened his mouth, but Jocelyn breezed back in, a silk scarf wrapped around her head and sunglasses on. She looked like a fifties movie star. Glamorous, sexy and downright tempting.

"Ready?" she asked with a smile.

He nodded.

"You can lock up, right, Chris?"

Her brother looked from one to the other, then said, "Yeah, I can lock up."

Kai took her by the elbow and led her out of the house and down the steps. A few minutes later, they were speeding down the road.

"Sorry about that."

He shrugged, trying to ignore the way it had made him feel.

"All of my brothers have been insane since I was in the hospital."

He nodded. "I said I understood. You know, when you were in the hospital, so was May. I know what it was like."

"Yeah, but I hate that they question my ability to be able to make my own decisions."

He shot her a smile. "We always secretly think that. We just keep it to ourselves."

She laughed as he'd hoped. "I always thought that. I figured they were always thinking it when I was at culinary school."

He turned onto Kam Highway and headed to Kaneohe. "I thought I would show you some pretty scenery, including where they filmed part of the first Jurassic Park."

59

She smiled. "That sounds fabulous."

"And then maybe we can hit some of the lesser-known beaches, just so you can get a feel."

She was quiet for a few moments, then asked, "Is there a reason you're doing this?"

He didn't answer as he passed a slow compact. "What reason would I have?"

Again, she paused. "Not sure."

He looked at her then and noticed that her smile had dimmed.

"Listen." He waited until he felt the weight of her gaze on him. "I'm doing this for a few reasons. One, you don't know anyone. Since I grew up here and know just about everyone on the island, I can't even imagine what you are feeling. Two, I know what it feels like to be the third wheel."

"Kai Aiona doesn't have a problem getting dates."

He shot her a quick look. "What do you mean by that? I don't even know you."

She laughed. "Honey, I grew up with three brothers and I work in an industry dominated by men. I know your species. I can tell you don't have too many problems getting dates. You're hot, you're nice, and I saw the way women reacted to you the other day on the boat. You have your pick of women."

He could feel heat in his cheeks, but he tried to ignore it. "Oh, I thought maybe you had heard rumors."

She laughed. "Cynthia said you do have a steady stream of women."

Anger surged, but he tamped down on it. The truth was, he had been that way for a long time. But something had changed in the last six months. Part of it was May's marriage, he knew that. But the other part of it had been Keisha.

"Truth is, I haven't had a date in over a month."

Silence greeted that comment.

"I'm telling the truth."

"Why?" she asked quietly.

He shook his head. Today wasn't supposed to be a day they told their sad pasts. It was supposed to be fun and relaxing. "It's a long, sad story."

"And you're not going to tell me."

"Why don't we save both our long, sad stories for later and just enjoy the scenery?"

She chuckled and he could feel her relax. "That sounds like a plan I can get behind."

five

By the time Kai pulled into a shopping center for lunch, Jocelyn was in love with Hawaii. Many people said they loved it, she knew that. More than one of her family had been here to visit Chris, but this was something different. It wasn't the kind of admiration she'd had the first few days after she arrived. It was like she had seen a different island. Gone were the posh hotels and all the touristy stores. It was different being with a local who knew how to show you everything.

"I have to say, I don't know if I am ever going to be able to leave."

Kai put the car in park then looked at her. "Why would you?"

She laughed. "That's true. I didn't know if I would stay here that long. Chris offered, and while he is a little overbearing, it is better than having the whole family breathing down your neck."

"I can understand that in a way. Hard though, since I still live with my family." He glanced at the shopping center. "Ready for some Hawaiian barbeque?"

She nodded. He slipped out of the car and walked around the hood before she had her scarf off her head. He opened the door for her. She stepped out and away from the vehicle and she felt her arm brush against his. She shivered and tried to ignore the heat that flared deep in her tummy. He shut the door, and it took him a second before he motioned for her to walk in front of him.

As she walked the through the door, the first thing that hit her was the scent of smoke. The next was the Polynesian flavors that she was growing to love.

"What do you recommend?"

He guided her through the crowd by placing his hand on the small of her back. It was a simple gesture, but still her hormones started to do the hula.

"Well, the pork is good, very good. You can get it with or without cabbage and some rice. And there's always musubi."

She looked at the pictures above the counter. "What's in that?"

"Your choice of meat with rice, wrapped in dry seaweed."

She wrinkled her nose. "No, thanks. I am not a seaweed girl."

"Ah, but they have it in SPAM."

She made a disgusted sound. "I don't understand the Hawaiian fascination with SPAM."

He laughed. "You might also like the chicken katsu."

Jocelyn nodded and stepped up to the counter, but Kai stopped her by placing his hand on hers. "No, I got this."

She opened her mouth to argue but saw his frown. "Okay. But next time, I buy."

He smiled. "Why don't you find us a seat?"

She glanced around and realized that it was getting more and more crowded. She found a booth in the back and headed over. She was just slipping into her seat when she saw Kai coming toward her. Again, female heads turned and admired. He was gorgeous, that was for sure. But he had something else that her brothers all possessed. A presence. Looking at him you knew he could take care of himself in a bar fight, but also take care not to hurt you. He was definitely the type of guy who used to make her go gooey.

Hell, used to? Right now, just watching the way his lips curled into a smile had her body heating, her heart beating so hard against her chest she was afraid she would pass out.

He set the tray on the table and slid in opposite of her. "What?"

She shook her head and tried to get her mind back to the now, but it was hard. It took every bit of her control to do it, but finally, she did it.

"Nothing. I think I am still trying to get over the jet lag."

He nodded. "It takes some people months to adjust to the time difference."

"So, are you going to tell me how Hawaiians got hooked on SPAM?"

"During World War II. They had a warehouse here and with supply lines sometimes in danger, it became a staple."

"I don't think I'll become a SPAM girl no matter how long I live here. I was amazed at the different varieties they had in the grocery store." She took a bite of her pork and hummed. "That is wonderful. Chris always says no one knows pork like Hawaiians."

When she looked up, she found him watching her in that way that made her stomach muscles tighten. His attention was on her mouth, and she wanted to say something, but the look in his eyes stopped her.

After a few long moments, he seemed to shake himself out of his stupor. "We'll have to get you to a real luau."

"I can't wait," she said digging into her food again reminding herself to tread lightly with him.

KAI PULLED into her driveway a few hours later and tried his best not to smile. Granted, he wasn't truly counting this as a real date, but if he had been, it would have been one of the best he had on record. He glanced at Jocelyn. Her head was back against the headrest, a smile curving her lips, her eyes closed.

"You're home."

She opened her eyes slowly and he felt the punch all the way to his gut. If she had been a pain in the ass or self-centered, he could have handled it. Knowing Chris the way he did, Kai had known she would be decent. In the small time they had spent together, he had found her to be absolutely beautiful on the inside as well as on the outside.

"Would you like to come in for a drink? I don't have much, but I do have some cookies."

He knew it was an invitation to thank him with only cookies. No matter how much his body was begging for it to be more. Still, he wasn't ready to let the day end.

"Sure."

He slipped out of his seat and walked around the front of May's car and opened the door. Slowly, in that unconscious sensuality that filled her every move, she rose. He knew it was just something that was innate in her, something that she couldn't help. It drew him to her. He always liked a woman who had no problem with her sensuality.

He followed her up the steps, cursing himself. He should have gone home and taken a cold shower. But instead, he was following her up the steps, her full ass swaying at eye-level. God, he could just imagine bending her over in bed, slipping into her from behind.

She stopped and he almost ran into her. That wouldn't have been a good thing, because he really didn't want her to know he was half-aroused. Again, the heat of her hit him, then the decadently enticing scent that he now associated with her. Before meeting Jocelyn, he would have never thought sugar and vanilla would be a turn on.

She unlocked the door and held it open for him as she stepped inside.

"Make yourself at home. I need to freshen up."

"Sure."

He toed off his shoes in the Hawaiian custom and started to look around the living room. Cynthia hadn't done much to change the small house since she'd moved in with Chris, but he could already see some of Jocelyn's things here. On the shelves there were pictures of her with her family, her brothers and what looked to be a younger sister. Then there was a picture of her, white coat, hat, her arms crossed over her chest, and a whisk in her hand. The smile she offered the camera said she was ready to take on the world.

"That was when I graduated with my masters."

He glanced over his shoulder. "Masters?"

She nodded. "Yeah. I wanted to be one up on everyone else."

He laughed and turned to face her fully. "Chris always did say you were a little competitive."

"That's what he says because he knows he couldn't make it through culinary school."

He frowned. "Really? I thought he had a college degree."

"He does, in business though. He would have never made it in a school where you are berated and belittled every day. Chris has a slow temper, but when it lights up, someone gets a nose broken."

He laughed. "But not you."

She shook her head, a small smile curving her lips. Damn, it struck him right there how much he wanted her.

"Oh, I got pissed, that's for sure. But for me, I wanted to prove that they didn't get to me, and I would succeed, despite what they do to you. It was a matter of pride and proving every one of the bastards wrong."

"Is it like *Hell's Kitchen*?"

She rolled her eyes as she crossed her arms beneath her chest. Luscious flesh rose above the neckline of her sundress. "Pfft, that's a cake walk."

He laughed at her dismissal.

"Why don't you have a seat at the bar here and I'll get us some cookies. What would you like to drink?"

He slipped into a seat and watched her move about the kitchen. He liked it. He wasn't some Neanderthal who thought women should be tied to the stove. In his family, if anyone thought that would happen, May made sure they understood she wasn't their maid or cook. He had been handling the kitchen duties even before his mother had been killed.

This was more. This was hers. She was in her element. She wasn't even doing anything big like decorating a cake, but it was the way she moved around that told him that no matter what, this was where she belonged.

"I'll just take some milk."

She smiled as she reached up to get a cup. The shirt she was wearing moved up, revealing her slender back. There was a dip in the small of her back that told him her full ass would be gorgeous in the flesh. He bit back a sigh. The woman was a work of art.

After filling up two cups, she joined him at the bar.

"There is nothing like milk and cookies," she said. "Mama always had some waiting for us when we got home. I know that most people go on and on about obesity today, but I think that comes more from sitting in front of the computer or TV. One or two treats a day won't kill you if you stay active."

He watched her dip the cookie in the milk then lean forward to take a bite. He drew in a deep breath and started to concentrate on his own treat and not the one sitting beside him.

"So have you decided what you wanted to do?"

She swallowed a bit of milk. "I think I'll work for Cynthia then decide. She's going to need some extra help because of the baby."

"Wait, she's pregnant?"

She smiled. "Yeah. I thought everyone knew about it."

He shook his head. "Nope." At least he didn't think so. Truth was, he had been so busy thinking about Jocelyn every day, he had avoided Dupree's. May had a full schedule this week, so she hadn't been by the family home much.

She gave him an evil grin. "Can you keep a secret?"

"Yeah."

"Chris is having sympathy morning sickness."

He laughed. "Oh, this is going to be good."

"You have no idea. I've been holding it over his head for days now. He doesn't want Malachai or Sean to know about it, let alone his friends here. Not sure he won't able to hide it much longer."

"May must not know."

She took another bite of cookie. "I doubt that. She is pretty sharp. And knowing her, she would use it the same way I am."

Kai nodded. "Blackmail. You sisters are all alike."

She smiled. "You know it."

AN HOUR LATER, Jocelyn followed Kai as he walked to the door, oddly deflated that he was leaving. The day had been wonderful, the company better, and everything in her wanted to invite the man back to her bedroom. She knew better, knew it was a bad idea. But even now, her body yearned to touch, to taste to—

"I'm glad you had a good time. Anytime you want another trip around the island, on or off my boat, just let me know."

"I will. I really had a great time today. Thanks."

He nodded and turned toward the door, but then paused. He turned around to face her.

"I promised myself I wouldn't do this."

Before she could comprehend what he meant, he stepped closer. Cupping her face, he gently brushed his mouth over hers. For a second, she couldn't think. Not out of fear but out of bone-deep surprise. She had thought he wasn't that interested in her, but now his mouth was moving over hers and she couldn't seem to think. So instead, she opened her mouth and returned the kiss. He groaned, the sound of it vibrating against her lips. She slipped her hands up his arms and over his shoulders. He stepped closer now, his entire body against hers. His heat enveloped her, pulled at her. She could feel the ridge of his erection against her belly and she wanted. Oh, God, how she wanted. His tongue stole inside, and she pressed closer. The taste of him entranced her as he slipped his hands down her body to cup her rear. Her nipples were hard, her body hotter than Louisiana asphalt, and she could feel the low hum of lust pulsing through her blood.

Then he was pulling away. She moaned in irritation. He chuckled.

"Jocelyn."

She slowly opened her eyes.

"I think it best I go now."

She frowned. "Why?"

"Because we just met, and it wouldn't be right."

Dammit, she hated good men. "Wouldn't be right?"

"Yeah. There are a lot of complications, and I'm not sure you are ready for something like this."

Irritation, embarrassment and a healthy dose of anger replaced the arousal he had so easily flared deep inside of her.

"So you don't want to finish? I think your body says another thing."

Her nasty tone brought her down to earth. What the hell was wrong with her? Here was a decent man, a nice one, who had gone out of his way.

She opened her mouth to apologize, but Kai stepped forward one more time, pressed his body against hers. Wet heat slipped down from her belly to her pussy and her body became one big pulse of need with that simple action.

"There is nothing more I would like to do than to turn you around and take you against this door. I have a powerful need for you that wouldn't be quenched with a quick, hard fuck. I understand that you might not understand, but I do have some decency and if there is anything between us, it isn't going to be a one-night stand."

He bit out each word. She could hear the desire threading every word.

She drew in a deep breath. "I'm sorry." She closed her eyes as shamed washed over her. She didn't need to be acting like this, like some kind of ass.

"Hey." His voice had gentled. She opened her eyes.

He cupped her face. "I want you. But like I said there are complications."

Pain and sorrow twisted in her chest. "I'm a basket case."

He shook his head. "That isn't so much of a problem, unless you mean by basket case you are going to go all Glenn Close on me and boil rabbits."

She snorted. "Not hardly. I have issues, but I am not a psycho."

He nodded. "And when you're ready to talk about them, you let me know. But the complications I'm talking about are our families. We're sort of entangled with May working for Chris. And I would hate to ruin a new friendship because we jumped into bed right away."

She should be grateful, but something inside of her was irritated. She squashed it. She knew she wasn't ready, knew that it could end up as a disaster if she tried.

"Now," he said, brushing his mouth over hers again. The simplicity of the kiss stirred more than lust. It had her heart quivering. "I have to go before all my good intentions are forgotten."

With that he opened the door. "How about dinner tomorrow night? My house."

"Safety in numbers?"

He smiled and she fought back a shiver.

"Hey, a guy has to be careful. Plus, I think my granddad has a crush on you."

She laughed. "Your grandfather has a crush on Dee. What time?"

"Six?"

She nodded. "Thanks again for the wonderful day."

He said nothing more as he shut the door and left her alone. She heard the car start up and drive away as she collapsed on the sofa. She leaned her head back against the pillows and closed her eyes. Damn, the man was lethal. Hot enough to burn her up, and just about sweet enough to make her melt.

She waited for the self-hatred to crash in on her. Ever since her issues with Greg, even thinking about a date had left her feeling lower than scum. Dr. Sawyer had helped her understand that none of it was her fault. Logically, she had known it. All of the gentle counseling she had been through had apparently worked. The guilt didn't come this time. This time, the only thing she felt was the fading hum of arousal and the knowledge that if she had a chance to go to bed with Kai Aiona, she would definitely do it.

"What bug's up your butt?" Vince asked.

Kai barely bit back a growl. But they had passengers coming on board. He was ready to explode. All day long Kai had been a pain in the ass, griping, bitching and snarling at everyone. And he knew the reason.

Jocelyn.

He never knew he possessed the kind of control he'd had last night. He had been within a second of talking her into bed. And he could have done it. He had been with enough women to know that she wanted it. But he felt she might have wanted it for the wrong reasons. And that had never really bothered him before Keisha.

"Hey, boss, why don't I take over the tour today?"

He nodded and said nothing else. He knew his crew was confused. Hell, he was confused. He didn't get tied up in knots over a woman he had just met. But he was. She had one of those soulful smiles that knocked him in the gut, and he knew when he got her into bed, that he wouldn't probably want to leave it for a week.

As he went through the preparations for the cruise, he started to think over his attraction, his need for Jocelyn. He knew better than to get involved with a woman who was hurting, who needed someone to prop her up. Keisha had been like that. Hell, a lot of women he'd dated had been like that. But until Keisha, it hadn't hurt when she decided to go on her merry way. She had told him two days before she moved back to the mainland. Two days. They had been dating for a couple of months, old high school sweethearts who had started dating again, and he had thought it would be fun to get to know the grown-up version. The problem was she had entangled him. He had been close to discussing moving in together when she'd told him she was moving back to the mainland.

Damn, he didn't want to deal with that again. Didn't want to deal with the fact he knew that Keisha ran off with a man she had just met and there were rumors about the guy, like he was into shady stuff and he liked to beat women. And he couldn't say anything because Keisha wasn't even a friend any longer. And he couldn't even blame her for using him. The truth was, until this year, he had never had a problem with it. He was known for mending broken hearts. But after Keisha... Well, he hadn't dated another woman since.

"You need to watch your temper around the crew," Vince admonished.

"Yeah, I know."

"You need to make sure that next time you go out with that hot woman from New Orleans, you get her into bed."

He glanced at Vince, then back down at his work. "I didn't say that was the problem."

"Son, all problems in life originate with women."

He chuckled. "Yeah, and how would you know? I rarely see you with a woman."

"Oh, I have women, but I make sure to keep them at a distance. You let them too close, they fuck you up."

He glanced up, intrigued. Vince had never been forthcoming with much of his background. Kai knew he'd been in the merchant marines, he was originally from Seattle, and he liked chili. Any more requests for information had been shut down immediately.

"Really? There's a story there. Who was the woman who taught you that lesson?"

A blush stole over the older man's face and Kai laughed. In all his time with Vince, he never thought to see something so, well, sweet on the hardened sailor.

"We're going to have to get you drunk and get it out of you." Kai shook his head. "And stop being a mother hen. I'm fine."

"If you're going to be in front of the passengers, you better tame that tongue of yours. Lots of kiddos on board today."

It always amused him that Vince gave him orders and always expected them to be followed. For the most part, they were. "Hey, who owns the boat?"

"You do, but it doesn't mean you know what the hell you're doing."

With that, Vince turned and walked back down the ladder, leaving Kai smiling after him. He was a pain in the ass, but Vince had taught him everything he knew about working on a boat. And he knew just what to say to get his mind off his troubles and back to business.

Jocelyn was a problem he would have to figure out later. He wanted her, but neither of them were ready. It was best to tuck his thoughts away until he could actually do something about it.

JOCELYN FROWNED at her brother as he matched it with one of his own.

"What do you mean you're going to Kai's for dinner?" he asked.

She shrugged. "He invited me to dinner with his family."

"And you just said yes?" he asked, his voice rising.

This was overboard, even for Chris. He had been bad since the incident with Greg, but this was downright freaky. She noticed one of the busboys slowly wander past. Mindful that some of the employees of his restaurant might overhear, she closed the door.

"Yes. I don't know a lot of people. And Cynthia gets up so early and with being pregnant, she needs her rest. I will be on the same schedule soon, but heck, I didn't want to eat dinner by myself."

Some of the fight seemed to go out of him. "I'm sorry I haven't been attentive enough."

She heard the guilt in his voice. Years ago, she would have used it to get what she wanted. She was a Dupree and they were a single-minded group. But she realized she felt better not dealing with him every day. Jocelyn loved being close to him, but she had her limits.

"No, it isn't that." She settled in the chair in front of his desk. "Don't worry. I don't need a sitter, Chris. I'm doing okay."

He studied her for a long moment. "Are you taking your meds?"

She shook her head and his frown came back. "I went off them before I came, with the help of Doctor Sawyer. She agreed I didn't need them. I have them if I should have to go back on, but right now, I am pretty happy with the way I'm progressing."

"I would feel better if you were taking it easier."

She snorted. "You would feel better if you could lock me in a room and have me stay there until you felt better about what happened."

"That isn't it at all."

She could tell from his expression he wasn't going to be able to deal with it. Not today, and probably not tomorrow. Chris hadn't been there, but he had known there was something wrong. He had called her a lot during all the problems and had even come to town. But being Queen Jocelyn, she had wanted to handle it herself. And paid the price.

"I understand you want to protect me, but I'm not fragile. I had a bad run of luck."

"You were almost raped. And by someone you trusted."

He didn't say it, but she could sense that he was blaming her. While she knew her brother loved her, and he understood it wasn't her fault, there was probably a tiny part of him mad at her for scaring the hell out of him. That she understood. It was his way of dealing with the fear, the worry. But she was sick of having that guilt heaped on her. They both needed to move on.

"I'm going to have dinner with Kai, his brother, his father and grandfather. And unless the family is into sharing, I doubt very much anything else is going to happen."

He crossed his arms over his chest. "I still don't like it."

She straightened her shoulders and lifted her chin. "I don't really care."

He opened his mouth when the door behind her opened. Cynthia stuck her head through the crack. "Is there anyone wounded in here?"

His expression softened when he looked at his wife-to-be. For the first time ever, a sharp shard of jealousy hit Jocelyn. It had never bothered her before, but now it hurt to see them together. She wasn't sure if she would ever have what they have, be able to trust someone the way they seemed to trust each other. She pushed it aside and turned to greet her savior.

"No, but it was close. I would have left my niece or nephew without a father."

Cynthia laughed and stepped into the office. "I thought it would be better if I came back here and saved him from himself."

Chris walked around the desk and took Cynthia by the elbow. The exaggerated care giving had Cynthia tossing Jocelyn an amused look. Jocelyn would've liked to help her, but with part of his focus on Cynthia and the baby, Jocelyn hoped he would lose some interest in her.

"I told you to nap today," he admonished.

"I did. What am I supposed to do? Stay in bed all day?"

"Yes."

She laughed as she sat in one of the chairs in front of his desk. "I am only six weeks pregnant. I think that is being a little overprotective. Besides, it isn't that much fun in bed by myself."

Chris glanced in her direction and she was sure she saw a rise in color in his cheeks. It still amused her that Chris would get embarrassed in front of her. Still, she knew a reprieve when she saw one. Jocelyn used Chris's preoccupation with his pregnant fiancée to slip out of there.

"I gotta get going." She leaned over and kissed Cynthia on the cheek and did the same with her brother. "I'll see ya later."

Before he could say anything, she slipped out the door and hurried down the hall to the restaurant. There she found May working the hostess stand.

"Hey, sistah. I heard you were being subjected to the males in my family for dinner."

Jocelyn sighed. "Does everyone know what I am doing? This is worse than New Orleans."

May smiled, her blue eyes dancing. "This is Oahu. Everyone knows everyone here. It's a little big town. And since a lot of the Hawaiians are related, even in the most convoluted ways, we all act like one big family."

"So you gossip about each other."

She leaned on the stand. "Got to have something to pass the time."

Jocelyn laughed.

"I guess the boss isn't happy with you dating my brother."

Jocelyn shook her head. "No. My brother isn't happy with me seeing any man."

May nodded. "I understand."

Irritation whipped through Jocelyn. "Why would you understand something like that?"

"I didn't say I agreed with it. I just said I understand. When you're the oldest, you worry. Kai is just as bad."

"Your brother? Mr. Laid-back?"

"Uh, yeah. I'm not sure, but I think he threatened Evan. Not really overtly, probably just something like, if you hurt her, I'll make the body disappear."

Jocelyn shook her head. "I can't see that. I mean, I can see that he would be protective and it is easy to see he has a good relationship with you."

May threw her head back and laughed. "I scare the hell out of him. As I do all of them, so if you go over there and the house isn't picked up, let me know. I swear, I moved in with Evan and they all think they can just forget about cleaning. It's embarrassing."

Jocelyn wanted to ask more about Kai, but she didn't want to push it. There was definitely something in his past that his sister didn't want to talk about, and at the moment, Jocelyn wasn't too sure she wanted to know. She wasn't sure she had the ability even to have a relationship.

"I gotta get going or I'll be late."

"Night, Jocelyn."

She headed out, enjoying the sweet breeze that surrounded her as soon as she stepped out of the restaurant. Growing up, she had liked being outdoors, but in recent years, she had been working so hard that she hadn't been able to enjoy it. But as she walked to the parking lot, she took in the approaching Hawaiian night. The days were gorgeous, but the nights, they left her sighing. No matter how hot it was, the cool air moved in, allowing her to watch the sun set, to walk down the street and enjoy the hum of the island life at night. There were times that nights during the summer had been unbearable when she had lived in Atlanta. She slipped into her car and was happy to roll the window down. As she headed down Kuhio Street, she smiled. God, was there another city in the world with as much natural beauty as Honolulu? Palm trees swayed from the gentle night breezes against the backdrop of high rises. But she never felt trapped here as she had in Atlanta.

She frowned when she came to a red light. She had never thought of her old home that way before, but now, she started to think of the last few months there and apparently she had. Was it that she didn't like living there, or the situation with Greg? It also had the double factor of harboring memories of Mike. The relationship had such promise in the beginning. They had both been new to Atlanta and had spent all their time exploring together. When everything had fallen apart, living in the city physically hurt. She couldn't go anywhere without seeing him and knowing what she had lost.

She waited for the pain and humiliation to hit her like it always did when she thought about Mike. But only the simple twist of loss was there. Did everything that happened with Greg amplify it? It saddened her that less than a year after her breakup from Mike she really didn't feel much for him. He was a man she'd loved, moved in with, and they had actually been discussing marriage. When Greg had started stalking her, the normal arguments couples have had amplified into screaming matches. For a short time, she had tried to do what Mike wanted. She attempted to prove his accusations wrong, but somewhere along the way, she had given up. Jocelyn had never been sure if she had given up too easily and had felt that maybe if she had worked harder at her relationship, they might have salvaged it. Maybe moving on, getting some distance from Atlanta had helped. She didn't know. There was probably no way to know for sure.

She thought back to the envy that had hit her when she saw Chris smile at Cynthia. She had never really felt it before, but now she had the first stirrings of a romance with Kai. There was a very good chance he was just passing the time with her, and well, it was not a hardship having a man like Kai pay attention to her. But she was starting to want something more. Not particularly with Kai, but just something more with her life.

The light turned green and she decided to push these worries aside. She had dinner with four very wonderful men to get to and she planned on enjoying it.

Kai smiled as he walked down the hallway to the kitchen. It had been a hectic day, mainly because he had pushed his crew to finish up early so he could make it back in time to clean up for dinner. But it had been hard to concentrate on anything but Jocelyn. He knew it was a mistake, but he just couldn't seem to get her out of his mind.

He stepped into the kitchen to find his father shredding the pork. He glanced over his shoulder and looked at Kai.

"That's what you're wearing to impress the girl?"

Kai looked down at his Hawaiian shirt and khaki shorts and frowned. "What's wrong with it?"

"It's a date. You should dress nicer."

He rolled his eyes. His father had been beside himself when he'd told him Jocelyn was coming over. Besides the fact that all the Aionas had missed having a woman in the house the last few months, Kai knew his father was getting ideas about him and Jocelyn. That wasn't good. He wanted the woman, had spent most of last night dreaming about her. But he wasn't sure if she would want a relationship, and he wasn't in the mood to save another woman.

You lie.

He sighed and tried to ignore his inner voice. He wanted Jocelyn, and he wanted her just the way she was. He knew he shouldn't want her this badly. It would be easy enough to find a woman for the night, slake his lust and go on his merry way.

But he couldn't do it. Every time he thought about doing it, the taste of Jocelyn's kiss came rushing back. It tripped over his nerve endings. Just thinking about it now had him humming.

His father gave him an odd look and Kai decided he needed something cold to drink. He grabbed a beer out of the fridge a moment before the doorbell rang. His heart tripped at the sound. Jesus. It was like he was fifteen and having his first lust-filled crush.

"What are you waiting for?" his father asked him.

Kai drew in a deep breath, ignored his father and walked to the front door. He opened it and she had her back to him. Life wasn't fair. If it was, he would not have to keep enduring that ass of hers. She was dressed in a red belted sundress with a halter top. It was simple but it did the most wonderful things to her body. It accentuated her small waist. She turned and smiled and something in him stumbled, then fell at her feet. She was lethal with that damned smile.

"Hi. I made it here without getting lost."

For a second he couldn't respond. His brain has shut down the moment he heard that slow, New Orleans' accent ripple over her words. It spoke of long, sultry nights, soft sheets and a willing woman.

"Kai?"

He shook his head, trying to regain his wits and not look like a fool. He smiled.

"Sorry. It was a crazy day. Come on in."

He let her walk by and did his best not to sniff. He lost that fight. She brought the night air and that same sweet scent he'd become addicted to since he'd met her.

He shoved his hand through his hair and released a

controlled breath. Damn woman was driving him insane, and from the innocent look on her face, she had no idea.

"Jocelyn," his father said as he walked down the hall. "I'm so glad you could find time to be with us."

His father gave him an odd look as he slipped his arm over Jocelyn's shoulders.

"I never turn down dinner with good-looking men."

His father laughed as he walked down the hall with her. Kai followed them, trying to calm his libido, but it did no good. Watching her as she walked, as well as the warm, affectionate way she talked to his father had more than just his body responding. And that was not good at all.

Drawing in another deep breath, he decided tonight would be a long night. The only thing he had to be sure of was not jumping over the table and kissing her.

As her laugh drifted back to him, he realized that would be harder than he expected.

SEVEN

Jocelyn smiled as Kai walked her to the car. "That was one of the most pleasant nights I've had in a long time."

He cut her a look that told her that he thought she was lying.

"Really. You have a pretty great family."

He shook his head. "They're crazy."

"Yeah, reminds me of my own. You might think you cornered the market on crazy with your family, but you haven't met the Duprees all at once. You will next month, so get ready."

He stopped when they reached her car. "That should be interesting. Am I going to have to deal with all your brothers warning me off?"

Embarrassment shifted through her, and not for the first time she wanted to shave Chris bald—including his eyebrows. She could do it too because her brother slept like a ton of bricks.

"No. Mama will be here so they'll behave."

He nodded but he looked unconvinced.

They reached her car and he shoved his hands in his pockets as if he were afraid he would touch her. That was interesting.

"I guess you have an early morning tomorrow?"

He nodded. "Well, probably not for a baker."

She laughed. "I'm starting work next week."

"You're going to work for Cynthia?"

She nodded. "Chris is trying to decide if he should disagree with me or thank me. It is kind of fun to mess with him."

"Yeah, and with the sympathy sickness, I'm sure he would like a break."

She laughed. "Have you told May?"

He shook his head. "I'm a man. I'm not going to side with the females."

"Hmm, I thought you liked females."

"I do. I just know how lethal they can be. May taught me that at an early age."

He said nothing more, just kept looking at her. She did her best not to fidget but it was hard not to. Even with only a dim streetlight she could see his gaze, the way it followed her lips. The man was going to turn her into a lunatic if he kept looking at her as if he were going to gobble her up.

That thought had heat rolling through her. Her nipples were tight against her lace bra, painfully erect. She shifted her feet and the lace moved against the sensitive flesh. God.

"Well, I guess I should get going."

"Yeah."

He placed a hand against the car behind her and leaned in. She didn't hesitate, didn't draw back. It was the most natural thing in the world to move into the kiss. Just like the night before, the moment he touched his mouth to hers, she lost every thought. They bled out of her brain and were replaced by the sheer pleasure of having his lips against hers, his tongue slipping into her mouth, and the feel of his body against hers. He slanted his head to deepen the kiss, slipped his arms to her waist and pulled her against him. The heat of him, the feel of his long, hard muscles against her, had her responding. She wanted, wanted him like nothing she had ever wanted before. Her body shimmered with need. She slipped her hands up his arms and over his shoulders, and just like the night fell into the kiss.

He was exotic to the taste, but so normal, so what she needed. She was trying to figure out a way to get him back to her house when a passing car honked their horn.

"Get a room, Kai."

He pulled back then, gently and with a regretful smile. "I guess we gave the neighbors a show."

Left unfulfilled again. "Not as good a one if that idiot hadn't beeped his horn." She couldn't keep the irritation out of her voice. It had been over a year since she'd had sex and months since she had wanted a man to touch her. And every time she got close, something happened. From the look on his face, he was going to go all hero on her. Dammit. God save her from men trying to protect her.

He stepped back, releasing her.

She said nothing for a moment, then, "You're not doing this because of my brother."

"No. I want to make sure you really want me."

Annoyance mingled with the unrelieved arousal. "What the hell is that supposed to mean?"

"I want to make sure you aren't trying to prove to the world that you're okay."

Embarrassment hit first. She knew that her brother's friends would have some kind of idea of what had happened to her, but if he knew this much, he knew. And he had been playing along to make her feel better. Dammit, it wasn't what she deserved.

She deserved someone who actually wanted to go out with her. Anger simmered, and as usual with her, she opened her mouth before she could keep herself from doing it.

"Fine. Don't worry. I won't bug you again, Kai. I understand that you were doing this out of the kindness of your heart, but you're free. I don't need someone who would be doing it as a pity fuck."

"Jocelyn—"

She held up her hand and marched around the hood of her car. He stood on the sidewalk, his facial expression blank.

When she reached her door, she drew in a deep breath. "I'm sorry."

He shook his head. "Don't worry about it. Goodnight, Jocelyn."

She wanted to say more, needed to, but she didn't. She had already said too much. Instead, she got into her vehicle and slammed the door. As she started the car, Kai walked around to the driver's side.

"I don't want you to go away mad."

She blew out a breath, trying to calm her irritation. She'd had a bad temper once upon a time. The meds she'd been taking had evened everything out, cooled any anger she'd once had to fight on a daily basis. It had been good for her for a while. After the attack, she couldn't handle the myriad of emotions that had crashed in on her. Finally, when she was ready to handle her life again, she'd been weaned off them. The deeper emotions had surfaced and controlling them was sometimes hard. Most of the time, she came out looking like an ass.

"No. I'm not mad. I'm frustrated."

"Believe me, I know the feeling."

She glanced at him then. "Why then?"

"I meant what I said. I want to make sure I'm what you want."

She nodded. "I'll let you know."

And with that, she threw the car into drive and took off. She couldn't deal with Kai or her need for him. Not tonight.

JOCELYN BIT into the sugary dough and hummed. When she opened her eyes, she found Cynthia smiling at her.

"I told ya. They are heaven."

Jocelyn chewed it, then swallowed before answering.

"Lord, that is good. You said they sell them with fillings?"

Cynthia nodded. "Not here, but some of the places around here have fillings, like you would in a donut."

Jocelyn sighed. "God, like I need another tempting morsel to make my hips wider."

Cynthia's smile turned into a grin. "Darling, you do not have huge hips. You have a gorgeous figure."

She rolled her eyes. "Said from the little petite beauty queen."

Cynthia laughed. "But not for long. I can't wait to get huge."

Jocelyn heard the yearning in Cynthia's voice and understood it. She had worked with a lot of pregnant women and knew before the tired feet and swollen ankles, many of them couldn't wait until they were showing.

"How is Chris doing?"

"Better now that he keeps saltines and water by the bedside." Cynthia studied her. "And stop laughing."

"I'm sorry. If you knew what a pain in the ass he was as a brother when I was growing up, you would understand. Hell, what a pain in the ass he is being right now."

Cynthia's expression turned serious. "You've been through a rough patch, hun. He's just worried about you."

It made her feel petty and small complaining. She knew what she had put her family through because of Greg. It also pissed her off.

"Are you sure he didn't warn Kai off?"

Cynthia cocked her head as she studied her. "Not sure. I don't think he has, and the truth is, if he did it wouldn't matter what he said to Kai. Kai marches to his own drummer."

Jocelyn sighed and looked away to study the busy street. Cynthia had met her up at the house and they had run into Wahiawa to do a little exploring. It was different from the cool urban streets of Honolulu. Locals mixed in with military because they were close to one of the Army bases. Here was what she thought of as the real Hawaii.

She felt Cynthia's hand slip over her fist. She looked over at her and saw sympathy. "What happened?"

Jocelyn sighed. "You're as bad as Shannon. She always knew when something was bothering me."

The moment she said it, Cynthia's eyes filled with tears.

"I'm sorry. What did I say?"

Cynthia picked up a napkin and dabbed her eyes as she sniffed. "You compared me to your sister."

"I told you I thought of you as my sister."

Another gush of tears filled Cynthia's eyes and Jocelyn started to panic. Cynthia must have seen it on her face because she laughed. "No. Don't worry. It still amazes me the way the Duprees all accept me."

Jocelyn knew of Cynthia's life before Chris, her hard father and the totally buttoned-down woman she had been before meeting her brother. It was hard to see that woman in the one who sat before her. She didn't wear a stitch of make-up, her T-shirt had seen better days, and the jeans she wore, well, they had too. On top of it, the black nail polish on her toes was another bit that didn't fit the old Cynthia image.

"Oh, sweetie. You know all the Duprees love you to pieces. If anything, you keep Chris in line."

"I try," she said with a watery chuckle. Jocelyn watched Cynthia pull herself together. "Don't think I'm done with you. What happened with you and Kai?"

She shrugged, not really sure. "We had a great day out. He showed me around the windward side. We stopped at an L and L to eat."

"Then what?"

"He kissed me."

Cynthia digested that for a second. "That's it?"

She nodded. "Then he said he didn't want to push, and left."

"Bastard," Cynthia said, amusement threading her voice. "Trying to be decent."

"Yeah. It gets worse. When I went to dinner at his house, I attacked him."

Cynthia's eyebrows rose to her hairline. "In front of his father and grandfather?"

She laughed. "No. When he walked me out to my car."

"What happened? Did you make out in the car?"

"I would have never guessed you for a voyeur."

Cynthia shrugged. "My hormones are going whackadoodle. I either want sex all the time, or not at all."

"Poor Chris."

"Since it's his kid, he has to deal with it. So what happened after the attack?"

"I kissed him, then he said he wanted to make sure I wasn't using him to prove something. And he didn't want to push."

"I hate when they go all hero on you." Cynthia sipped her tea. "But then it makes me all gooey."

Jocelyn sighed, thinking about the incident and the tone of his voice. "I know."

"Have you talked to him since then?"

She shook her head. "I thought about it, but then…" She let her words trail off.

"You didn't want to chase after him and look pathetic?"

Jocelyn nodded. "I kissed him right there that night and he rejected me."

"Was he good? I always thought Kai would make the world melt."

Jocelyn laughed. "Yeah, well, I think I melted right there, on the sidewalk. I could feel it all the way to my toes."

Cynthia sighed. "I had a feeling. He's always sort of been this good guy, but you could sense the naughtiness beneath. Sort of like Chris."

"Oh, ew, don't compare them. That's icky."

Cynthia laughed. "No, I just mean both of them are pretty responsible, and I think not because they have to be. Well, Kai had to a bit. His father and grandfather aren't the best people to be in charge of three kids."

"How old was Kai when their mother died?"

"Hmm, May was twelve, so I guess Kai was thirteen, fourteen. At the most, he was fifteen. I know he dropped out of school a year or so later to work the docks."

"Really? I would have thought with his mind for business he would have at least had some college."

"I have a feeling there wasn't enough money. Plus, May has always said that Kai was a guy who didn't go for college. He didn't always do that well in school, never applied himself. But they needed the money more than likely. May's mother didn't have much of an insurance policy. They were probably in a bind financially. And as I said, being responsible, Kai understood. Of course, he did pretty good for himself."

Jocelyn felt for him. Not pity, but a sense of admiration. As a boy, he had made choices that some men wouldn't be able to deal with. And dammit, it made her like him even more. She had never had to make the choice of what she wanted to do in life. Her family had made sure that she could make it to culinary school without question.

"He seems to like his job now."

"Yeah, he does. And it doesn't hurt that he's a charmer. But I have a feeling working the docks at the age of sixteen isn't fun. Now he has the money to do what he wants, but before, it had to have been hard."

Jocelyn groaned. "And that just makes him even more fascinating. Dammit."

Cynthia laughed. "He probably knows something happened with you. Chris was gone and well, everyone knows it was for you. That's why he's being so gentle."

"That's what I was thinking."

"Plus, he is still trying to recover from Keisha."

The way she said the woman's name made Jocelyn think she didn't like her.

"What happened?"

"Well, Kai is sort of, I hate to say it, but he's always been a good rebound guy. Not that he minded from what I could tell. But Keisha...they had dated in high school—remember I am getting this all secondhand from May."

Jocelyn nodded.

"Anyway, they went to prom together the year after Kai dropped out. Then they sort of went their separate ways. Keisha went back to the mainland for a while, then came back. Anyway, she was dating this real loser about a year ago, then she kicked him out. May was pretty sure the guy was abusing her. Dee thinks so too. Kai and Keisha started dating and I don't know, Kai...I have never seen him fall like that. I mean, he dated women, but he started bringing her to our get-togethers, like the one the other night."

"What happened?"

"She dumped him. Dumped for some asshole she just met. Keisha has a lot of issues, one of them being that her father was pretty much an abusive asshole. So, she is once again dating an abusive asshole, just like her father. But as you can expect, Kai took it really hard. He didn't really date for months. Well, you were probably the first date he'd had in a while."

"I would think a man like that would have his pick of women."

Cynthia nodded. "Yeah. That's why I know he was hurt. So he might be a little leery of rushing in. Especially since you're Chris's sister and May works for him. Sticky situation. Like I said, good man."

Jocelyn sighed. She couldn't win.

"What?"

"Well, I can't get a scumbag to leave me alone, but a good guy goes running for the hills."

Cynthia shook her head. "No, honey. It might be he's looking for something more and wants to take his time."

"What if I can't give him more?"

Cynthia sighed. "Then I guess you have to take your time. No one expects you to have the answers, Jocelyn."

"I feel like I should, that I should be able to figure it out."

Even she heard the frustration in her voice along with a hint of whine. She hated it. Hated the feeling of not being in control.

"Are you okay? I know the last few days have been hard on you."

Since she'd started working at Cynthia's, Jocelyn had been dealing daily with some of her new anxieties. It had been hard the first day, the initial fear of so many people. But the work had soon filled her day and she found herself lost in her love of baking.

"No, in fact, I think it saved me. And it helped make sure that your child has a father. Chris was going to drive me nutty with his mothering."

Cynthia laughed. "Well then I have done my part. Just remember that he loves you. And, remember, Kai does like you. He definitely has a thing for you from the way he watches you. Both of you just need to figure out where to go from here."

"I hate waiting. So I guess I will console myself with another *mallasada*. Want one?"

"Always."

"GOOD MORNING, JOCELYN."

Jocelyn smiled as she turned and found Mr. Aiona standing on the other side of the counter. He had been in each of the six mornings she had opened the bakery.

"Good morning, Danny. I would say I was surprised to see you here, but that would be a lie."

He chuckled. "How about you say you're happy that I am here?"

She couldn't help but let her smile widen. As each day had slowed down between the breakfast and lunch rush, Danny would come in, coax her into a cup of coffee and conversation. Cynthia came walking from the back, a little pale.

"Are you okay?"

She nodded. "Yeah. Better. Don't tell your brother."

"As long as you lie and tell him I didn't know when he finds out. And you know he'll find out."

Cynthia waved that away but they knew she was right. "Hey, Danny. How are you doing today?"

"Fine, just fine. Is that *keiki* giving you problems?"

"Just in the mornings. Doc says I'll be fine. You can take your break now, if you want to, Jocelyn."

"Sure. Want to try my first attempt at *malassadas*?" she asked Danny.

His eyes lit. "Oh, yes. One of my favorite things."

She hid a smile. Everything she offered was one of his favorite things. She had a feeling that since May had moved out, Mr. Aiona had been a little lonely for companionship. Kai and Danny, Jr., his younger son, were busy with their lives.

They took a seat outside to enjoy the cool morning air. Jocelyn breathed it in and hummed. "I don't think I have smelled air so sweet as here in Hawaii."

"You got that right. Can't stand the mainland myself."

"Your son told me the same thing."

He nodded. "Smart boy."

Jocelyn sipped her coffee as she watched Danny bite into the *mallasada*. His eyes widened. "Oh, that is good." He nibbled at it. "Very good."

"I'll pack you some up for your father."

Danny nodded. "He'll enjoy that. I take it you're enjoying your time in Hawaii?"

"Yes, sir. It's so...relaxed here. No one is really fussy. It reminds me a lot of New Orleans that way."

He studied her for a second. "You miss home."

"Yeah. But I haven't lived there in years really. I spent most of my time in Atlanta. But now I am trying to understand just why I did that."

He smiled at her, the same kind of fatherly smile she got from her own father. But there was a hint of Kai there in the way his eyes sparkled. "Sometimes it is the journey that's important."

She nodded. "Maybe you're right. I kept saying things like that to myself when I was in the hospital."

Understanding softened his features. "Yeah. But we went through that too. I have always thought that things happen for a reason. May's problem brought her and Evan together and now he is in our lives." She heard the love there, for May and Evan. "You're here because of what happened in Atlanta. Sometimes we have to be reminded of precious things."

She didn't hesitate as she leaned forward and kissed his weathered cheek. His face flushed. "You are the sweetest man. How come some wonderful woman hasn't snapped you up?"

"There was only woman for me."

The sureness of his voice told her it was nothing but the unvarnished truth. She felt her heart turn over in her chest.

"She was very lucky."

He shook his head. "You have to understand. Every man is lucky if they find a woman to put up with them."

She sat back and allowed the conversation to move to something lighter and enjoyed his company. As Danny said, sometimes the journey is as important as the destination.

"HEY, Kai, is that your father at the dock?" Tommy asked.

Kai looked up and saw his father standing there. A rush of fear came first. His grandfather hadn't been doing well, but then he took in his father's smile and his relaxed posture and released a breath.

"Yeah. I wonder what he wants."

After they got the boat docked, he left his crew to handle the fishermen and their catches for the day.

"What're doing down here, Pop?"

"Nothing much." He handed him a bag. "Been by Cynthia's."

He opened the bag and a fresh wave of sugary sweetness hit him. "*Mallasadas*. I didn't know Cynthia was making them."

"She's not. Jocelyn is."

Just the mention of her had Kai's body reacting. His heart slipped into an erratic rhythm and his palms grew damp. He glanced at his father and felt a bit of alarm when he took in his knowing look. To cover his embarrassment, he motioned for the bench.

Once they were settled his father said, "I don't know what's wrong with the men on this island. That girl has been here a few weeks and she doesn't seem to go out much."

Kai shrugged. "She has to be into Cynthia's early."

"There are enough of them buzzing around her."

He glanced at his father. "What do you mean?"

"There are a lot of guys who pop in for lunch. Cynthia said there's been a rise in businessmen showing up for lunch."

Anger and jealousy hit him square between the eyes. He pushed it aside. "Jocelyn's a good-looking woman."

"And sweet. Why aren't you dating her?"

"I'm not having this conversation. She needs time to put her life back together again, Pop."

Sympathy and understanding filled his expression. "She's not Keisha."

"I know that. But I just...just let it go."

He nodded. "Okay. If you want to give up a beautiful woman like that, you go right ahead."

"I'm not giving her up. I'm giving her time."

His father frowned. "What the hell for?"

"She needs time to adjust to her new life."

"Pooh. Your generation thinks too much. Not enough action."

He laughed. "I remember one time you complained that I did too much action."

His father sighed. "I'm giving up. I have to go pick up your grandfather who spent the morning probably getting more action then either of us has gotten in a good long while."

Kai laughed. "How about we eat out tonight at Duprees?"

Something came and went in his father's eyes, but he couldn't tell what it was. "That sounds like a plan."

eight

J ocelyn smiled at Chris as she watched him try and hold
back another wave of nausea. "Stop it. I told you I would
beat you if you made fun of me."

"You shouldn't be such a puss then," Evan said from the
chair next to her. She laughed.

"Yeah."

"You both suck. And Evan, I hope you get this in spades
when you and May decide to have children."

Evan leaned back in the chair and stretched his legs out.
"I'm made of sterner stuff than that, son."

Chris rolled his eyes. "So what are you two here bugging me
for?"

Jocelyn cocked her head in Evan's direction. "He's here
because May's working. I'm here because Cynthia said we were
all going to have dinner here."

Her brother's skin paled.

"Well, maybe I'm just having dinner. Did she just get sick
and that's why you are?"

He held a napkin over his mouth. "Yeah. The doctor said she was okay."

She wanted to give him more of a hard time. He deserved it for some of the things he pulled on her, but she heard the worry there, the fear. She reached across the desk and patted his hand. "I'm sure her doctor's right. I worked with a sous chef who spent all nine months sick. It was really hard on her, but she delivered a very healthy baby. Everything will be all right. Why don't you and Cynthia go home?"

"Yeah. I'll have dinner with Jocelyn," Evan offered.

Surprised, she looked over at Evan. "Sure. That'll be great."

Chris sighed. "I really wanted to spend the night together, but I just don't have the energy to do it."

Fifteen minutes later, she and Evan were sitting in a booth together.

"I didn't realize he would worry."

She snorted and put the menu down. "He is a worrywart, but I know that's normal. She has been sick a lot, although not more than some. I just dread the birth. Can you imagine? He's going to drive us crazy."

"Are you going to be here then?"

It was a good question. She had a feeling that her family had been dancing around it not wanting to ask. "I think I might. I'm still not sure yet."

He nodded. "No reason you have to decide right now."

She sent him a repressive look. "That's what you non-planners always say."

He laughed. "Yeah, Micah gets after me, but then he worries enough for both of us." He studied her for a second and then said, "If you would like a free pass to Rough 'n Ready, I can give you one."

Evan was Micah's not-so-silent partner. They owned one of the premier BDSM clubs in the entire US.

She felt her eyes widened then she laughed. "Oh, God, no."

He frowned. "I don't want to pry, but Chris told me a little bit."

Her laughter died.

"Not that much, but if you have issues, you can work them out there."

She sighed. "Not my thing, really. Even before Greg and the mess. I explored it, but it's just not my thing."

He nodded. "Just let me know. We do have a therapist who works on and off there if you need to talk."

It was so sweet, and again, she was thankful for Chris's friendship with Evan. It was like getting another brother without all the issues she had with her blood brothers. She leaned across the table and kissed his cheek.

"You really are sweet."

His cheeks reddened.

"Moving in on my man, Jocelyn?" May said with a laugh.

Jocelyn turned to face her and felt her words dry up in her throat. Behind her stood the rest of the Aiona clan, including Kai.

She swallowed. "Naw. Just thanking him for being so sweet."

May looked at her husband. "As I live and breathe, are you blushing, Evan?"

He grabbed May by the waist. "Make sure you behave or you will get payback."

"Only if I'm lucky."

Evan kept one arm around May and looked at his in-laws. "What are you doing here?"

105

"Night out on the town," Mr. Aiona said. "Hello, Jocelyn."

"Hello again," she returned with a smile.

"So are you going to buy your family some dinner tonight?" he asked Evan.

The smile Evan gave his father-in-law was filled with affection. Evan had never really known his real father and his mother had been a drug addict. Each time Jocelyn saw him with the Aionas, she could sense the connection between May's family and Evan.

"Do I have a choice?" Evan asked.

Danny shook his head. "Not really."

Feeling like an interloper, she started to move out of the booth. "Why don't I let y'all have a family dinner? I was supposed to eat with Chris and Cynthia, but she was kind of queasy so they went home."

Danny patted her hand. "No, you join us. We need a lovely lady to make dinner enjoyable."

She glanced at Kai but his face still held no expression.

"Sure, darlin'. May says we always need a woman around to keep us in line," Evan said.

"Okay." She didn't dare look at Kai while they were hustled out to a bigger table. Of course, Danny worked it so that Kai and she were sitting together.

"I'm sorry," he said, leaning so close she could feel his heat. It took all her control not to lean closer and rub up against him.

She looked up. "What for?"

He grimaced. "I know this wasn't in the plans for your evening."

"What, dinner with five very attractive men." She smiled at the table, then looked at Kai again. "I wasn't raised to be a fool. And only a fool would turn down this kind of invitation."

He opened his mouth to say something, but May walked up to the table and started taking their orders. Jocelyn settled back and decided she would make it through the night without jumping his bones.

"Kai, why don't you walk Jocelyn to her car," his father said.

Heat filled Kai's face. God, his family never had any kind of subtlety.

He noticed that Jocelyn paused in pulling on her sweater. But other than that, she said nothing.

"If Jocelyn doesn't mind."

She gave him an innocent smile. "Why would I mind?"

She stood and then went to the end of the table where his father sat. He stood and she gave him a hug. "Thank you for the wonderful evening, Danny."

"I paid."

She sent Evan a snarky smile. "Yeah, well, who would have paid if we had been alone?"

"You're as bad as your brother so I know I would have."

She laughed and walked to him. She leaned down, hugged him from behind and kissed his cheek. Kai knew it was a brotherly affection, but he felt a jab of irritation when Evan whispered something in her ear. Nodding, she stood up and looked at him.

"Ready?"

He nodded and followed her through the door. It was hard to concentrate on putting one foot in front of the other. It had taken every brain cell he had to concentrate since he'd walked into Dupree's and seen her sitting across the table from his brother-in-law. What she was wearing didn't help. As usual, it was bright. Neon pink sleeveless shirt, tucked into very worn blue jean shorts. And those legs...they went on for fucking forever. He had been dreaming of them wrapped around his waist.

"I hope you don't think I planned what happened tonight."

His brain wasn't really working so it took him a minute to figure out just what she was saying. It was kind of hard to form words when there was no blood in your brain.

"Uh, I didn't think that."

She relaxed as she walked beside him. "Good. While I've gotten to be very fond of your father, I would never work with him to trap you into spending time with me."

He looked at her profile, trying to figure out if she was joking. When he saw nothing on her face to tell she was, he shook his head.

"You don't have to trap me to spend time with me."

They reached the rental he recognized. She rummaged through her purse.

"You could have fooled me."

"What the hell does that mean?"

She pulled her keys out of her purse and frowned at him. "You haven't called me in over a week. I kissed you and you gave me the crap about me being ready."

He almost reacted to the anger but he could see the pain beneath it. He had never expected to hurt her.

"I told you to let me know when you were ready for more."

She narrowed her eyes and even in the dim parking lot light, he could see her irritation. "Really? So you're not avoiding me?"

Of course he was. If he had spent any time with her, he

wouldn't have been able to keep his hands off her. But he knew better than to tell her the truth.

"No."

"So you just avoid the days I'm working at the bakery?"

He couldn't think of anything to say.

She brushed past him to the driver side of the car. "Never mind. Listen, I am not some kind of charity case. I won't bother you anymore."

He grabbed her arm and she froze. He silently cursed himself, but he wasn't going to back down. He eased her around to face him.

"I didn't say I didn't want to spend time with you."

"Then what? What the fuck is up your ass?"

"If I spend any time with you, I want my hands on you. Hell, I was close to touching you under the table at dinner. It's embarrassing."

He let go of her and paced back and forth, frustration riding his back. He had made sure to leave her alone, let her have her time. And what did he get? Nastiness. Women never change. They say they want a good man, a nice man, and you give them that and get shit.

"So you've been avoiding me because you're afraid I'm not ready?"

He stopped and looked at her. "You just got here, and let's be honest, I've heard some of the stuff that has been talked about. Hard to avoid. So yeah, I was trying to be good and not bother you."

She let out a frustrated sound that sounded more like a growl than a sigh. "I am sick to death of people deciding what is best for me."

"I—"

"No. You can hide behind that, you can say that you were trying to give me time, but you weren't. Let's be honest. You can't keep your hands to yourself? Like I'm so pathetic I can't say no?"

He opened his mouth but she rolled right over him. She grabbed his shirt and yanked him to her. Before he could react, she was kissing him. Her tongue slipped past his lips, slid over his and then she pulled back. She was breathing heavily, her breasts rising above the neckline of her shirt.

"Ask me now. See if I want you in my bed tonight."

"Jocelyn."

"Yeah. Never mind. At least I don't have to hear excuses from my batteries."

With that, she marched to her car, slid in and started it. He was still trying to get his brain to function again and she was pulling out of the parking lot, almost running over his toes in the process. By the time he could, he cursed.

"Having trouble with the ladies?" Evan asked.

Fuck. "No."

Evan chuckled as he walked toward him. "I came out here to keep an eye on you, but apparently I need to keep an eye on Jocelyn."

Kai closed his eyes and willed embarrassment away. Damn, nothing like having another man witness Jocelyn bitching him out.

"Have you really been avoiding her?"

Kai opened his eyes. "Yeah. She's...well, she's a little too much to resist."

"I wouldn't know."

He gave his brother-in-law a strange look. Evan shrugged.

"She is like a little sister to me. I never had one, so I sort of adopted both her and Shannon."

"Is Shannon any sweeter?"

"A bit, if you don't mind her mouth. Woman is always telling people what to do with their lives. But you have to give Jocelyn some credit."

"What do you mean?"

"Before she came here, she was barely surviving from what Chris told me. She wasn't acting like her old self."

"And now?"

"Well, you are starting to see why she was good at her career. She did have the nickname of Queen Jocelyn when she was in the kitchen. She knows how to handle herself."

Kai blew out a breath.

"You are going after her, aren't you?"

Kai looked at the exit to the street, "No. Not tonight. She needs some time to cool off."

Evan slipped an arm over his shoulder. "I'm not going to push, but I will say you have a lot to learn about women."

J ocelyn came awake on a gasp. She gulped in deep breaths of air as she tried to calm her heart. Sweat dripped down her spine as she shivered. It had been bad, so vivid. It had been weeks since she'd dreamed of the attack. She rubbed her arms, trying to push away the memory of what it had felt like when Greg had griped them, leaving marks.

"Just a dream, Jocelyn." The words came out as if a prayer. She closed her eyes, pulled in a deep breath, then released it as she opened her eyes again.

She swung her legs over to the side of the bed. With more strength than she thought she had, she pushed out of bed and padded barefoot to the bathroom. She turned on the light and winced as the bright light pierced her eyes. Damn. She couldn't go without light. It was a moonless night, and she didn't know the house well enough yet. She rubbed her temples as her head started to pound. Of course, a headache. Just what she needed. Not that she'd had a wonderful evening to begin with. First her embarrassment with Kai, then her dream.

She opened the medicine cabinet and grabbed some aspirin.

She dropped two into her hand, then placed the bottle back on the shelf. It sat next to the prescribed meds. One was to make her happy, to forget everything and just float through life without any worries. She had been on them until recently, until she'd convinced her doctor she hadn't needed them anymore.

Maybe she did. But she couldn't take going through life in slow motion. She hadn't had any panic attacks while on them, but she hadn't felt anything else. She would rather live in terror than exist like that.

She filled a cup with water as she thought about the sleeping medication also in her cabinet. She could take it tonight, but it would make it impossible for her to make it to work tomorrow. She needed a good eight hours of sleep before they wore off. And she didn't want to take something that made it hard to wake up. She didn't want to exist in that dream.

While staring at the bottles, she tossed the aspirin in her mouth and then drank the water. It was a tiny bit of defiance, or maybe she was trying to test her resolve. She would not succumb to them. Not tonight.

She turned off the light and walked back into her bedroom. A glance at the clock told her she wouldn't be getting much more sleep, so she went into the kitchen to start coffee.

She waited at the counter and thought about her embarrassing behavior. What the hell had she been thinking? She hadn't been.

The problem was she felt smothered. Everyone was mothering her, handling her with kid gloves. It had fit her when she was on the drugs. It hadn't bothered her at all. Hell, she couldn't feel a damn thing on them. So what was a little overbearing from well-meaning friends? And she had needed it if she were honest with herself. Mike had been a complete ass about the whole thing, and when she had needed someone to lean on he had left. It wasn't the way she had expected that relationship to work out. In fact, they had talked of marriage, but that had dissolved because of Greg's behavior. Of course, if there was one thing that came out of what had happened, it was learning what a complete loser Mike had been. He might be considered a celebrity chef, but he was an ass in her book.

But some of her dreams had disappeared when he'd left... They had talked of opening up a restaurant together. She sighed, but that idea was no longer viable. Right now, she didn't know what she wanted to do with the rest of her life. And that was fine. Even if she had to repeat that phrase a few times.

Mike had tried to mend fences months later after the attack. While she had accepted his apology, she has sent him packing. She didn't need a man who wouldn't stand by her when she needed him.

Her coffee machine dinged that it was ready and she filled a cup and walked into the small kitchenette area. The dream might have cropped up because of her behavior. The rush of emotions could have brought on the nightmare that had plagued her after the attack. Or could it be that she was sliding? She waited for the regular panic to fill her, but it didn't. In fact, the only thing she felt right now was well, being embarrassed as hell.

She closed her eyes and the image of Kai's expression when she left him standing in the parking lot came to the forefront of her mind. Damn, she had been such a bitch. It hadn't really been his fault. No, partially it was his fault.

Did she really believe the bullshit that he didn't come around her because he couldn't keep his hands off her? She scoffed and took a sip of coffee. As she went over the night in her mind, little things came to mind. His knee kept brushing against hers, and every now and then he'd seemed to lean closer to her. Maybe there had been a little truth in that. He had been beyond aroused when she'd kissed him. She'd felt the long, hard length of him through their layers of clothing.

She sighed. It still didn't make it right that he was giving her space without telling her, other than the cryptic comments. That pissed her off. Maybe it was because people had been walking on eggshells around her for months. Even before Greg had attacked her, she had become a raving bitch. Hard not to with her boss and mentor hassling her, making her life a living hell. Not to mention Mike accusing her of cheating. She had started to implode and had gone full diva on more than one employee.

With a sigh, she realized she would have to apologize to Kai. It was going to suck, but she would do it. Then, the ball would be in his court.

"HEY, Kai, isn't that your lady?" Vince said. For the second time in as many days, there was someone waiting for him when they docked. This time it was Jocelyn. Damn, she looked good. She was wearing another halter dress, this one in sunny yellow. It was cut down far enough to give him a fantastic view of the swell of her breasts. He sighed.

"Damn, if you aren't going to date her, do you mind if I call her?" Tommy asked.

He resisted the urge to break Tommy's legs and then beat him over the head with an oar. Barely.

"No. You stay away from her or I'll kill you."

Tommy said nothing for a second, then, "That's not like you at all."

As he walked away, Kai realized his friend was right. From the first day on his boat, he had been territorial about her, and that wasn't something he did. Even with Keisha, he hadn't been like this. There was something about Jocelyn that made him want to protect her. It wasn't because she was weak, or the fact that she had been through a rough patch. No, there was something primitive beating through his blood that urged him to conquer.

She smiled at him as he hopped off the boat.

Mine.

It was the only word that came to mind when he saw her smiling at him, with the sunshine on her and the fresh scent of the ocean surrounding them.

"Hey," he said. Yeah, he was a Don Juan with the words.

"Hey."

"I didn't expect to see you today."

She made a face. "I came to apologize."

He wanted to laugh because she sounded so non-apologetic it was funny. But he didn't.

"For what, pray tell?" he asked innocently.

"I brought you cookies," she said abruptly.

"Jocelyn."

She sighed. "I'm sorry I yelled. I guess I am still adjusting to life without meds."

He nodded. "So those for me?" he asked.

She gave him a small container. "I just wanted you to know I wasn't really mad at you. I just...I hate the way people tip-toe around me. If you were just taking me out to be nice, I would rather you would be up front."

"No. I want you. I thought we had established that already."

She took off her sunglasses. "Then when you think you can handle it, you come to me. I'm not going to chase after a man. I pretty much let you know I wanted you."

Damn, she was blunt, and if that didn't make him like her even more. And he wanted to take her back to her place, make slow love, fast crazy love, whatever until they wore themselves out. But he knew that he needed space, they both did.

He leaned forward and he hated the wary look in her eyes. He would do his best to fix that, but he thought a few days might be best.

He gave her a simple kiss, just barely brushing his mouth over hers. When he pulled back, he said, "I will definitely be calling you. Just...I need a few days."

She nodded. "Maybe we both do. Bye, Kai."

He watched her walk down the pier to the parking lot to her car. His heart was beating fast, his hands sweating. Shit, all he had done was give her a little kiss. Not much of one.

But it had his body begging to follow her. And that more than anything else scared the hell out of him.

"IF YOU CAN'T DO your job right, then maybe you need to find another one," Kai said, his irritation with his skipper over-riding any better sense.

His crew looked at him like he had grown a second head

and Kai knew why. He didn't threaten to fire people, especially in front of the rest of the crew. He felt, rather than saw the crew drift away as Vince walked toward him.

"Boy, you need to go after that girl."

"I'm not your boy."

"Yeah, I thought you were a full-grown man myself. Hard to tell by the way you've been behaving the last few days. But I told you a few days ago to go after her. Sitting on your ass isn't going to get you anywhere."

Kai looked over the expense reports for the last month and the numbers bled together. "Get off my back."

"I will if you start running your ship right again. I don't want you on this ship until you fix your temper."

Kai tossed an evil smile over his shoulder at Vince. "You're ordering me off my ship? Are you forgetting I'm the boss?"

"No. But I don't want to unleash you on the public right now."

It irritated him. Damn woman. He had told her they needed a few days, and he had given her that. He had never been a man who liked to deal with high-maintenance women, but he had a feeling that Jocelyn was just that. Besides the fact that she liked things her way, she had been through a rough patch. That added to the baggage he wasn't equipped to handle. In the end, there was a very good chance both of them would end up being hurt.

It didn't mean he could keep himself from wanting her, and it didn't mean he liked waiting to make sure it was the right time.

"Listen, if the woman doesn't want you, then find someone else. Do something, but don't come back until you get out of the mood you're in. It has gotten worse every day this week."

"Okay."

He turned back to the paperwork and he felt Vince's gaze on his back. "What?"

"Just want to be sure you won't show up at the dock in a few minutes."

"No. Going to finish the paperwork."

"Well, then..."

"Just go. I'll kick your ass later."

The older man chuckled. "As if you could. Later."

When he was alone, Kai realized just how much of an ass he had been over the last week. He had grown nastier every day. So much so, his crew was barely talking to him, and May had said she disowned him. Evan had taken pity on him and taken him out drinking the night before. There had been more than one willing woman there. Tourists with time on their hands, wanting a good memory of the islands. With each and every one of them he had wanted to snarl. He thought he might have at the last one.

With a sigh, he realized he didn't have a choice but to go see Jocelyn. It was that or drive himself and everyone he cared about insane. He checked his watch, then decided to call someone who knew Jocelyn's schedule and would help him out.

Jocelyn finished decorating the cake and stood back to admire it. The cake was simple, just a child's birthday cake, but it had been fun to start decorating again. She loved everything in baking, but decorating cakes had been a joy she'd had since she was a girl. As she progressed through school, she had realized that not many people had the innate ability to handle cakes. They weren't hard, but there was a thin line between gorgeous and trashy. Most people didn't know how to handle it.

"That is so cute," Cynthia said as she stepped up beside her. "Winnie the Pooh was always one of my favorites."

Jocelyn nodded. "Mine too. I hope they like it."

"Are you kidding me, they'll love it. I think we are going to gain more and more business with you around, especially after my wedding. That is going to get you tons of referrals."

"I thought it was going to be small."

Cynthia smiled, her dimples in full force. "It will be, but you are still learning about living here. It is all one little big town. Everyone knows everyone else."

"May said something like that."

Cynthia nodded. "By the end of July, you will probably be so booked up I will have to hire another baker."

"Why don't you go home and check on Chris."

While Cynthia's morning sickness hadn't been too bad, Chris's was getting worse. Something that most of the people who worked for him were taking great joy in.

"I think I'll take you up on that. They already paid and they know to knock on the front door. She should be here in the next thirty minutes."

Jocelyn shooed her out of the bakery a few minutes later and smiled at the silence. She had been busy since she'd had started working a week ago and she loved it. Every day she was up before the sun rose, but she had spent her afternoons enjoying Hawaii. There was nothing like walking on the beach every day, taking in the scenery, smelling that sweet sea air.

It was more than that. At first, she had issues with personal space. Hawaiians tended to stand closer than some other nationalities, and she had been bringing her pills with her to work, just in case. She did not want to have a breakdown in front of everyone. But she hadn't needed it. Most of their customers were some of the sweetest people she'd met. They were open and friendly, but not prying as many of her friends back in New Orleans had been.

Jocelyn was bagging the plastic pieces for the cake when she heard a knock at the door. She turned, a smile on her face, and froze. Kai stood there. It had been a week since she had seen him. She walked to the door and unlocked it. "Hey, we're closed."

He gave her an odd look. "That's good because I didn't come here for the food."

She felt heat fill her face. "Come on in. I'm waiting for someone to pick up a cake."

He stepped inside, then around her as if trying not to touch her. It embarrassed her that he was acting like she might jump him if he touched her. Just because it was true didn't mean she would act on it.

After locking the door, she turned and found him watching her. Those green eyes hid secrets that she wasn't sure she would ever know.

"What did you want?"

His lips curved. "I know you have tomorrow off, so I wondered if you were up to a beach day."

She frowned. "How do you know I'm off tomorrow?"

His cheeks reddened. "I might have called Cynthia."

For a moment, she couldn't respond. Seeing a big, strong guy like Kai blush boggled the mind. Then, in the next instant, she realized what he had said.

"Cynthia didn't say anything to me about it."

"Yeah, I asked her not to."

She crossed her arms beneath her breasts. "I meant what I said the other night. I don't need anyone taking pity on me. I can make my own friends."

"I don't remember you saying anything about friends."

She opened her mouth.

"And neither did the neighbors across the street sitting on their front lanai."

She covered her face with her hands. "Oh, God."

"Or my father, who heard through the open window. Not to mention Evan who saw what you did to me in the parking lot of *Dupree's*."

Embarrassment shifted through her. That temper would be the death of her someday. She lowered her hands, but before she could apologize there was a knock at the door. She glanced over her shoulder and saw Mrs. Blakenship who had ordered the cake.

"I have to give her the cake."

"No problem. I'm good at waiting. Take care of her, then we'll talk."

She nodded and hurried to help the customer. She pushed her nerves aside and concentrated on her task. Then she could deal with Kai.

KAI LISTENED to Jocelyn speak to the older woman, who kept thanking her for the beautiful cake.

It took her more than ten minutes to get the woman out of the bakery and lock the door.

"I was thinking we could go on up to the North Shore. It is nice this time of day. There are jellyfish warnings over here."

She started when he spoke, then she looked up at him.

"Are you okay?"

"Yeah." She shoved a hand through her hair and sighed. "That woman can talk."

He laughed. "She wasn't that bad."

"I'm not used to handling customers. But Cynthia looked tired and well, Chris was..."

She trailed off and he started laughing. "Sick. Yeah, May is giving him a hard time, but I told her to be careful. One of these days it could bite her in the ass."

She cocked her head as she studied him. "Why are you here?"

Because I can't stay away. That would be the blatant truth. He couldn't admit it to her. Other than the fact that his crew was ready to stage a mutiny, there were other things. He went to bed with her on his mind, woke from dreams that tormented him.

"I wanted to clear the air."

"I said I was sorry. I thought we had a truce."

Her back was ramrod straight again, and he could tell by the set of her shoulders that she was irritated. Embarrassed too. Well, too bad.

"Yeah, I heard ya. Then, you know, there's the thing about going to the beach."

She sighed. "I know you're trying to be nice, but you don't have to."

He would think she was stupid if he didn't know her so well. "I know. But I want to."

She opened her mouth and the frustration he'd been

suffering from came up. "Listen, I asked you out. I stayed away a week. This is not about pity."

The room was silent after he finished and she pursed her lips. "Okay. You want to follow me up?"

"I thought you would take pity and drive me in your cute little car."

"You saw it?" she asked, and he nodded. "I couldn't resist. Convertibles in Atlanta seemed like a waste to me, but here, it's almost a necessity to enjoy a drive. I loved May's so I couldn't resist. Let me double check the back door."

He nodded and waited, trying to calm his heart. It was beating out of control and his body hummed with arousal. He hadn't touched her, hadn't even gotten that close to her since stepping in the store. But it apparently didn't matter. Just being in her presence had him rock hard. He hoped she didn't notice.

"Okay, let's go."

She turned and locked the door and he shoved his hands into the pockets of his shorts. He didn't need to touch her, not here, not now. There was a good chance that he might just take her up against the window of the bakery.

"I'm parked around the corner," she said with a smile.

They walked in silence for a few moments.

"Are you going to tell me what this is about?"

"It's about a day together, just like the others."

"Oh."

She sounded disappointed.

"No plans, just enjoy."

She smiled. "I usually plan out everything."

He nodded. "Just like May. I like to take life as it comes at me."

She reached her car and unlocked it. Once they were both inside, she said, "Total opposites."

"But it can be fun."

She laughed. "You're right about that."

He settled back and let her drive.

THEY SNAGGED some fish tacos on the North Shore, then headed to Kaiaka Bay Beach. It was normal, or at least would have been if the underlying sexual tension wasn't driving her slowly insane. Yes, she had felt this with other men, but not as over powering. Why was this man so tempting to her? He stretched out beside her and sighed. She bit back her own.

"I do like a day at the beach with nothing to do."

She cocked her head. "You know, you might be able to pass yourself off as a loafer to other people, but not to me. You're a businessman at your core."

He squinted at her, then closed his eyes and settled his head on his arms.

"I don't know what you mean."

It was something that had been nagging at her for days. Her brother had called him laid-back, but Kai wasn't. Not by a long shot. That is what he let everyone else see.

"Who's Keisha?"

"Been asking around?" he sounded amused, but not angry.

"No. Your father mentioned her."

That had him frowning and squinting up at her again. "My father? When did you talk to him?"

She laughed. "Your father comes in every day I am at work."

He grunted and closed his eyes. "Oh, yeah. He's mentioned it. He has a crush on you."

Thinking of the older man and their daily talks had her heart warming with affection. "That's okay. I have one right back."

Silence reigned and she looked out over the scene in front of her. Soft, blue-green waves rolled in gently as kids played in the sand. She watched one toddler run out into the waves, her peals of laughter when the wave knocked her down ringing through the air.

"Keisha and I dated for a while."

She glanced at Kai whose eyes were still closed.

"I guessed that." She shrugged even though she knew he couldn't see it. "It isn't like I don't think you have a past. I definitely have one."

"Dad thought we might get serious. Hell, everyone thought we would at least move in together." He didn't have to say anything for her to know he had thought about taking another step with Keisha. And from what she had heard about him, Kai wasn't the kind of man who got serious.

She picked up some of the warm sand and watched it as she let it fall out of her hand. It was softer than the sands along the Gulf Coast.

"I was living with someone a year ago."

She didn't see but she sensed him still next to her. "Yeah?"

She nodded. "When...when things started happening with my boss, he thought I was cheating on him."

"Ass."

She glanced at him as she continued to play with the sand. "Why do you think that?"

"I don't know you as well as he should have, and I know

that you would never cheat. You might dump a guy and break his heart, but you wouldn't cheat. Not your style."

"Well, gee, thanks. I think."

He laughed. "No. I think it says more about a person if they're truthful."

She studied him for a second, the sounds of the beach patrons dimming as she pulled together her nerve.

"You like honesty?"

He nodded.

"Then why don't we go back to my place?"

He studied her. "Why?"

"That's an odd question."

He shook his head. "No. I think it is an honest question."

"You want to know the truth. For the first time in nine months I want a man to touch me, and I want you to be that man."

His gaze darkened, his face flushed. The air between them grew thicker.

"Okay." He stood and started walking away.

"Wait," she yelled as she jumped up and caught up with him. "Just like that?"

He turned and faced her. "You were honest. You didn't tell me you wanted me forever, that you needed me more than your next breath. What you said was, you wanted me. That's enough."

ten

K ai could tell by the way she moved she was nervous. She should be. Beyond the fact that she apparently hadn't had sex in at least nine months—he was betting it was actually longer—he was barely holding onto his control. If she had lied, if she had tried to make light of the situation, he might have been able to walk away. But he recognized the need in her voice. It wasn't just sex. It was survival. He followed her into the small house, shut the door and leaned up against it.

She set her keys up on the kitchen bar, then turned to face him. He said nothing as he tried to control his thoughts. He was here, he would get to have her, and dammit, it was pretty much what he had been dreaming of for the past month.

"Did you want something to drink?" she asked.

He shook his head, still saying nothing. He was afraid to. He knew she wanted this, wanted to feel again, but there was something nasty beneath his surface that was egging him to conquer. That was not what she needed now.

"I..." She sighed. "I don't know what to say."

He smiled and pushed away from the door. As he

approached her, he noticed little things. Her breathing was fast. The pulse in her neck hammered and her eyes were dilated. He took her hand and drew her behind him as he continued on to the bedroom.

He tugged her through the doorway, then led her to the bed.

"Take a seat."

"I'm not completely sure." She opened her mouth to continue, but he had had enough. His nerves were riding a thin line. He leaned down and kissed her. Simple at first, but next, as usual, the heat between them exploded. He leaned against her and she fell back onto the mattress. He enjoyed the feeling of lying on top of her. His cock pulsed and his need roared through him. But he needed to make this good, needed to do this for her. He pulled away and kissed his way down her neck. Her skin was naturally sweet and warm from the sun. God, he would never get enough of her, of touching her...tasting her.

He licked at the pulse in her neck and felt it flutter and then speed up. He unbuttoned her top, kissing the skin he bared as he spread the fabric apart. The pink bra cupped her breasts and with each breath, flesh rose above the confines. The soft color contrasted with her cocoa-colored skin. It had a front closure, thank the good Lord, so he pressed it. Her excited gasp sank into his skin. He was trying to keep it together, trying to take it slow. But he didn't know how the hell he would keep it together. His cock was hard, ready, willing. Hell, he'd been ready since the moment he met her.

"Kai."

Her soft voice, filled with southern need, caught his attention. He looked up at her as he bent his head to her breast. Those gorgeous eyes of hers were half-closed, a flush brightened her cheeks and he could feel the arousal slipping past her barriers. Without breaking eye contact, he pressed the flat of his tongue against the tip of her nipple and gave her one, long lick. She shuddered so slightly he would have missed it had he not been so close to her. He continued kissing down her body, enjoying the sweet, salty taste of her flesh. As he inched down her pants, he sighed when he saw the pink scrap of lace. Women with a love of naughty panties had always been his personal favorite. It showed him that on some level she had dealt with the sexual threats her boss had made. There was something else there. Something in the way she dealt with him that told Kai she hadn't had a man since. He couldn't fight the totally primitive need to be the first for her again.

He eased the panties down her long legs. She wasn't a skinny woman, and he liked that. Her legs were muscular, but not too hard. There was a feminine curve to her thighs, he thought as he licked her flesh.

She shifted her legs closer together, but he didn't want that. He needed to see her as much as he needed to taste her.

He gently pulled them apart and sighed. Her pink lips were wet, glistening with need. He smelled the pungent fragrance of her arousal. Slowly, he dipped his head, then pressed his mouth on her pussy. She seemed to freeze for a second. He slipped his tongue along her slit, then she shivered and relaxed against him.

The flavor of her exploded over his tongue, over his taste buds. Salty sweet, and just as sassy as her personality. He took her clit between his teeth and she moaned. It sounded strangled as if she were holding back. And that gave him a mission. He wanted her so lost in the moment that she was screaming his name. He slipped a finger into her pussy and groaned as her muscles clamped down tight on his digit. She shifted closer, slipping her hands through his hair, molding her fingers to the back of his head. He continued to tease her clit, alternatively sucking then blowing on the small bundle of nerves. He could feel her orgasm approaching as he slipped another finger into her core.

"Come for me, Jocelyn."

Frustration shimmered in the air around her as she fought for release. He could physically feel it as she tried to come.

He moved his fingers in and out of her, then took her clit between his teeth again. In that next moment, she spasmed, and a long, throaty moan vibrated out of her throat as her inner muscles clamped down hard. He lifted his head and watched. She threw her head back, exposing the column of her neck. At the same time, she arched her torso, causing her breasts to thrust up in the air.

Long moments later, she relaxed against the bed. He slipped from the bed, tore off his shirt and then started to unbutton his pants. It was then that he noticed that his hands were shaking. He drew in a deep breath, closing his eyes and trying to remind himself to go slow. It was hard to do because every instinct he had told him to take her fast and hard. He could do that later. Now he needed to make sure he didn't spook her.

When he opened his eyes, he noticed that she was watching him with a small smile curving her lips. Her gaze traveled down his body, and he shouldn't have blushed. He had spent his life in Hawaii, on the beach, half-naked. But as her big green eyes took in his body, heat blazed a path along with her gaze. He didn't know if he had ever seen a woman look at him quite this way. As if he were a treat for her to enjoy.

Her gaze finally lifted to his face and she laughed. "Are you blushing?"

He cleared his throat and this should have been a turn off. But hearing her joy, seeing the sparkle in her eyes, made him smile.

"It's just...well, the way you're looking at me."

She scooted to the end of the bed and placed her feet on the wooden floor in front of him. She spread her hands over his chest, smoothing over his nipples.

"I never dated a guy who had a nipple ring before." She smiled up at him. That and the teasing in her voice had his cock twitching. "I sort of like it. I also heard you have more interesting piercings."

He rolled his eyes. "A couple of my friends started that rumor years ago. I can't believe anyone still talks about it."

She slipped her hand over his shorts, her fingers caressing his shaft through the fabric. Damn, he should have worn underwear today.

He closed his eyes again and bent his head back. He was close, closer than he expected to be after a little oral sex with her. But there was something in her, something he wanted to touch...that had him very close to the edge.

Without saying a word, she slipped the fabric of his pants down. He opened his eyes as his cock sprang free into her hands. He wanted to tell her no, that he didn't know if he could control himself. When he saw her face, filled with excitement and lust, he couldn't bring himself to do it. He felt her breath tickle the head of his cock, the moment he felt her tongue slide over the very tip. Over and over she licked him as she moved a hand up and down, pumping him. With every stroke she pushed him closer to the edge, but he couldn't seem to form the words to tell her to stop. It felt so damn good.

She licked down one side of his cock, then up the other as

she slipped her hands down to his sac to caress him. He allowed it only for a few moments before he pulled her away tumbling both of them back on her bed. He stretched out on top of her, wanting nothing more than to dive into her. But he cursed when he realized he needed a condom. He jumped off the bed, slipped off his shorts the rest of the way, grabbed condoms out of his wallet and tossed it behind him.

He tore one condom package free and dropped the rest on the bedside table. Ripping the foil, he had the condom on in seconds and was back in bed with her. She giggled, something that sounded so young and carefree, it squeezed his heart. He'd heard her laugh since he met her, but nothing that sounded this free, this thoughtless, this wonderful.

He slipped up her body, positioned his cock at her entrance and entered her in one hard, swift thrust. She drew in a breath and he silently cursed himself. She wasn't a virgin, of course, but she was tight, and she had said it had been awhile.

Looking down at her, Kai brushed her hair away from her face. Her eyes were closed.

"I'm sorry," he said as he started to nibble at her bottom lip again. Damn, he loved her mouth.

She said nothing but slipped her hands up over his shoulders to his head. She pulled him down for a hot, carnal, devastating kiss.

"No reason to be sorry," she whispered the words against his mouth.

He lifted himself off her, taking her generous hips into his hands as he started moving. God, each time he slipped into her core, tiny muscles grasped, pulling him tight, pushing him closer to his orgasm. But he wanted to see her come again. He wanted to watch as she lost herself in pleasure.

It didn't take him long to build her back up. Soon she bowed beneath him, her breasts thrusting heavenward. He couldn't resist. He dipped his head, taking a nipple into his mouth as he felt his orgasm move over him. With one last hard thrust, he came, his orgasm seemingly lasting forever. He collapsed moments later.

"I might be dead," she said, her voice filled with lazy satisfaction.

"You and me both, sistah," he said as he raised his head. Her face was flushed from their lovemaking and the scent of it lay heavy in the air. He leaned up and kissed her nose.

"Thank you."

"For what?" she asked.

"For letting me be the first one."

She smiled. "Thank you for wanting me."

"A man would have to be dead not to."

He gave her another quick kiss on her nose as he moved away and got rid of the condom. He slipped back in bed and pulled her against him.

"Rest," he said, giving her another kiss on the top of her head. Kai couldn't seem to quit kissing her. It was then, with Jocelyn snuggled up beside him, that he realized that he might just be in over his head.

And for the life of him, he didn't give a damn.

JOCELYN WOKE up in slow degrees. She could still feel sun on her face, so she knew not a lot of time had gone by. She closed her eyes and smiled. Her body felt well used, and she couldn't help but feel smug that she had finally stepped over the invisible line. Dr. Sawyer would be so proud.

She felt Kai run a well-callused finger down her arm. "I thought you might get a little more rest," he said, his voice deep, resonant, downright sexy.

She opened her eyes and turned to face him. Damn, he was gorgeous. She'd had a lot of men in her time, but none of them had affected her the way that Kai had. And sadly, she barely knew him. Was that the reason he intrigued her so much?

"Why do you think I need sleep?"

His mouth turned up at one corner. "Because I know you've been up since O dark thirty. And you have to get up early again tomorrow."

"It's early. And remember, I don't have to work tomorrow. I've got a lot of time for sleep."

His smile turned carnal. "Yeah, but I wasn't planning on letting you sleep much tonight."

A bolt of heat lanced through her. "Yeah?" She slipped her arm over his shoulder. "And you thought I would let you spend the night?"

He leaned closer and took her bottom lip between his teeth. "I thought I might be able to convince you. I was also hoping for some dinner."

The look he gave her was equal parts innocent and naughty. She felt her heart shiver but she pushed it aside. Or pretended to.

He skimmed his hand over her hip, then up to her breast. She bit her lip to try and keep from moaning. He kissed her chin.

"Why do you do that?"

She opened her eyes. "What?"

"You try and keep from showing any pleasure. Why?"

She shrugged. It had never been a problem before, but now, it felt somehow...wrong. She knew the psychological reasons. Her doctor had warned her about them. But she was too embarrassed to admit it. Anger flashed in the depths of his eyes, but it disappeared so quickly she thought she might have been mistaken.

"Well, I think I might have to do my best to get you to make some noise." The mischievous tone sank beneath her skin. There was enough heat in it to have her head spinning.

She slipped up on top of him. She wanted to give in to him. It had been about a year since she had even thought of taking a man to bed, and Kai had made it wonderful for her again. Sitting up on him, she felt his cock pulse beneath her.

"How about a little fun, then dinner?"

He smiled and then groaned when she rolled her hips. "If this is an example of your ability to recover, I'm definitely going to need some food soon."

She laughed. "You're so easy."

He slipped his hand between her breasts to her neck and pulled her down to him. "With a woman as beautiful as you, it is pretty hard not to be easy."

He kissed her then, slipping his tongue between her lips. Heat that had been simmering blazed. If she thought about it, she would probably be worrying. A man had never gotten her this crazy so fast. But there was something so freeing about being with Kai.

By the time she pulled away, she was already aching, her pussy wet, needy. She reached over to the side table and grabbed a condom from the stack he'd brought. She sat there, looked at the four or five condoms.

"I don't know if I should be impressed or worried."

His hands were on her hips and she felt his cock twitch again.

She scooted down as she ripped the package. She decided to be mean and take her own sweet time rolling the condom down his impressive length.

By the time she had, his fingers were digging into the sheets.

"I am going to pay you back for that."

She said nothing as she moved back up him, leaning over him, allowing her breasts to rub against his chest. There was something about him that made her feel powerful, in control. She rose to her knees and then slowly eased down on his cock. Inch by inch, she sank down, enjoying the way he filled her. Once she finally had all of him in her, she started to move. Up and down, slowly at first, just enjoying the way he groaned her name as she flexed her hips each time she slid down.

Soon though, she felt her orgasm approaching, the telltale sign of a rush of heat. Kai leaned up to take a nipple in his mouth and tugged it between his teeth. She shivered and increased her movements, frustration starting to build. She needed to come, right now. As Kai teased her breasts, he slipped a hand down to her clit and took it between his fingers and squeezed. It sent her hurdling over the edge into the hot abyss of her orgasm. He rolled them over, switching their positions and pulled himself up to his knees as he started to thrust into her. Before she was recovered from her first orgasm, he sent her into another one.

When she opened her eyes, she found him watching her with an intensity that scared her. But for some odd reason, she couldn't seem to look away. Even as her body was recovering from her second release, she felt him building her up again. Fear and arousal intertwined in her chest. She wanted to stop it. He must have sensed it, because he leaned down and kissed her.

"Don't. Don't hide. Not from me, not from this."

She wanted to. She didn't like the loss of control. But as he slammed into her hard one last time, she felt herself dissolve into pleasure. This orgasm was more powerful than the first two and she screamed his name. She closed her eyes as he groaned her name. A moment later he rolled them over, and she snuggled against him.

His skimmed his hand down her spine and said nothing as they watched the last rays of sunlight slip away.

eleven

"This is possibly the best tasting peanut butter sandwich I have ever eaten," Jocelyn said before taking another big bite.

Kai smiled, enjoying her happiness. They had fallen asleep after the last bout of love making and woken up ravenous. It had taken a lot for him to drag his ass out to the kitchen. But once there, he knew it had been worth it.

"I might have to have another one," he said.

Her eyes widened. "You've already had two."

"I have to keep up my stamina. You'll wear me out otherwise."

She laughed. Just that made his heart jerk. He couldn't keep himself from falling deeper beneath her spell. Damn, she was something. He had known a lot of women, been with more women than he could probably count. But this one, she did something to him. Just seeing her smile, hearing her happiness, made the world brighter.

"Kai, is something wrong?"

He shook his head, trying to gather his thoughts. He

couldn't be in love with her. Nothing was settled, she was still trying to get her life back in order. And he knew for a fact that she wasn't ready for it any more than he was.

"Kai?"

The worry in her voice pulled him from his thoughts. He noticed she was frowning at him so he covered up his feelings and smiled.

"Nothing. Just a little more tired than I thought I was."

She nodded but didn't look like she believed him. She rose from the table, and he snagged his arm around her waist and pulled her onto his lap.

She snuggled close to him and then smiled up at him. "Is there something you needed?"

Your love.

There was another small jolt of pain to his heart. He couldn't ask for that when he knew he wasn't able to promise he could give it in return. "Yeah. Another sandwich."

She giggled as she rose and smacked his hand. "I should tell May that you are trying to order me around to get you food."

But she went about making him another sandwich.

"What do you think your brother is going to do when he finds out?"

She shrugged. "Not really any of his business."

She set the sandwich on the plate in front of him and then sat back down to drink the rest of her milk.

"Of course it is. You're his sister."

She rolled her eyes. "Ugh, you brothers are all the same, but no, it isn't. I am an adult who can make her own decisions. Been doing it for some time now."

He reached out and cupped her cheek. "He's just looking out for you because he loves you."

Her expression softened. "I know that. But it can be a bit smothering, especially since I'm used to dealing with it at a distance."

He rubbed his thumb over her cheek. "I can talk to him if you want me to."

"God, no. Let me handle Chris. It isn't like he can order either of us around."

He dropped his hand and started eating his sandwich. "It seems odd to me to have that many miles between you and family."

She cocked her head and studied him. "I guess so and that is important here, right? I mean, I hear people talk about *Ohana* and how the family is the most important thing."

He shrugged. "It is a way of life that you probably can't find on the mainland."

"It was different when Chris came over here. I never thought he would last." She shrugged again. "I don't think any of us thought he would. We do have a very close family, but he fell in love with the island. I could see it the first time he came back for a visit. It was under his skin. A part of him." She sighed. "I can understand that."

He heard it there in her voice. Some people could live on the islands their whole lives and never really appreciate them. But some people, it tugged at them, at their hearts and they never left. Which would suit him just fine to have her stay.

"How do you like working at Cynthia's?"

"I like it. I wasn't sure if I would. I was so used to working in a high-pressure job, and while we have schedules and all that, the pressure I had in Atlanta isn't there."

"Along with your problems." The moment he said it, he wanted to call back the words. Her expression blanked and she blinked at him. Dammit, he couldn't help it. He wanted to know everything about her, the good and bad.

She sighed. "Yeah. I was at the top of my game when I tumbled down."

"You didn't tumble. You were pushed."

Her eyes widened. "I guess you could say that. I guess you want to know more."

"Only what you want to tell me."

She laughed, but this time there was little humor in it and he hated it. He took her hands into his.

"I'm serious. I don't have to know anything you don't want me to. But I think you need to say it."

She nodded. "You might be right. I didn't really talk to anyone about it. I mean, I had to give a statement to the police and all, but I didn't tell family about it. I couldn't." She sighed. "I met Greg when I was working on my Masters. He was brilliant and he usually picked one student each year to mentor. I thought I had made it when he chose me. He didn't usually pay attention to the bakery students. Greg was usually all about the grill."

Of course, the bastard had chosen Jocelyn. He remembered the picture he'd seen a few weeks ago, her smiling face. She would be tempting. She was beautiful, and the attention of someone like him would definitely be more than a young woman would be able to ignore.

"Did you have a relationship with him?"

She shook her head. "God, no. He was...like one of my brothers. Or I thought so at the time. We worked a lot together and he was the one who suggested Atlanta at first. I wasn't too keen on it. I like big cities, but I tend to like them a little slower, like Honolulu. Atlanta is, well, it's crazy. I didn't know he'd planned on moving there himself. It just had seemed so natural when he contacted me six months later and asked if I would be interested in his new restaurant."

"Of course," he said, barely keeping his sarcasm at bay. She tossed him a look that told him to settle down.

"It wasn't like that. Or I didn't know it was. He hadn't tried anything while I was at school, so I thought he might not be interested in me."

"Really? I would say he would have to be dead."

She snorted. "No. Greg was white and he never messed with any of the black students, so I thought maybe he didn't like black women that way. I assumed that he saw me as a colleague. Stupid."

He shook his head and took her hands in his. "No. If he had been a decent guy, you would have been right. It has nothing to do with you and everything to do with the bastard."

She nodded. "Yeah, Doctor Sawyer said as much."

"Your therapist?"

"Yeah."

"When did it go bad?"

"Not for another six months. He was pretty cool with his advances, I didn't even recognize them. I was living with Mike at the time so I wasn't even paying attention to men in that way."

"Mike?"

"Yeah, Mike Sanders."

"Mike Sanders, the big celebrity chef?"

She nodded. "That would be him."

Irritation and a good deal of jealousy burned in him. It was stupid, he knew that, but still part of him hated that she had been involved with anyone. Especially someone so successful.

"Ow, Kai."

He realized he had been squeezing her hand. He relaxed his fingers and then rubbed hers. "Sorry."

"About six months into the working relationship, Greg's wife moved out."

"He was married?"

She smiled at his outrage. "Yeah. And with her went a lot of his money. She had financed a lot of his restaurant, and when she left she cut off his money flow. She apparently found out he'd been sleeping with their twenty-one-year-old nanny."

"The guy is a predator."

"Agreed. I didn't know this at the time. Some of it came out later when he was arrested. The prosecutor dug it up on him. She said we had to establish a pattern."

She paused and he realized she was scared to tell him. Reliving the horror of what she had been through might be too much for her.

"You only have to tell me what you want."

She smiled. "I know you probably hate to hear it, but you are the sweetest man."

She leaned forward and brushed her mouth over his.

"If it gets me kisses like that, I can deal with being called sweet."

"Yeah. I bet." She sighed and then straightened her spine. It intrigued him even more. He had been known as a man who helped women through their heartaches. But this woman went beyond that. He didn't want to save her. She could stand on her own and dammit, that made her irresistible.

He took her hand in his and threaded his fingers through hers. "Go on."

"When I began to work for him, the problems started. He

became a little too...touchy. I mean, he had always been a guy who did that, to everyone, men and women. He was part Italian and that is what he blamed it on. And at first, it didn't bother me. You've seen how Chris and I are. We are a demonstrative family so I didn't have a problem. Until Greg. It became kind of creepy.

"I just blamed it on the stress he was under. I wasn't stupid. I knew he was a cheater. Hell, everyone at the school knew that. But I had always thought he had an arrangement with his wife. They pretty much had their own lives. Maybe having someone in their house was a little too much."

She drew in a breath. "Things went downhill fast. He started showing up at places I was at."

"Like where?" A cold chill filled his stomach.

"First, it was really casual. Running into each other at the mall or at the theater. Then it was all the time. He would just show up at my house with no notice. Especially the nights that Mike was working."

"What did Mike do about it?" he asked.

She looked at him, a frown turning her lips down. "What do you mean?"

"Mike. You were living with him, in a serious relationship, so what did he do?"

She made a face. "He accused me of cheating on him and moved out. I learned later that Greg had pretty much insinu-ated that he and I were sleeping together."

Still, in Kai's mind, Mike should have known better. More than likely there had been signs of the harassment and the asshole had just ignored them. How a man could think Jocelyn would cheat was beyond him.

"Then it got worse. Greg just became very scary. So I quit. It wasn't something I was used to doing, but I couldn't take it anymore. Greg did everything he could to make it impossible to get another job. He put out the word that I was horrible. That when my work had started to fail, he had fired me. Which wasn't true, but he had a little more of a reputation than I did, and why would he lie?"

"Because he's a disgusting bastard."

She smiled at him. "The exact same words Chris used. The only kind of job I could get was at a grocery bakery. I figured I would move as soon as my lease was up and maybe by then Greg would get over the fact that I had turned him down. But it didn't work out that way."

She hesitated and a tremor moved through her as if she were reliving the terror.

"You don't have to tell me." He had wanted to know, but it was physically hurting him to hear the story. He could detect the pain in her voice, the shame she was still dealing with, and he felt useless. There was nothing he could do to stop the memories from hurting her.

She looked up at him, determination in her gaze. "No. I think I do."

He nodded but said nothing else.

"He found me one night at work. I had stayed late to finish up and one of the idiot stock boys let him back to see me. He tried to get me to come back to the restaurant. He offered insane things. Twice the amount he was paying me before I left. A car. Anything. Then he tried to get me to admit to being in love with him. Talk about delusional, it was really crazy. I ordered him out of my kitchen and he lost it."

She closed her eyes and he squeezed her hands. "The same stock boy who had opened the door for him dragged him off me. I have never seen anyone that crazy." She opened her eyes and he saw the haunted memories there, simmering with the unshed tears. "I mean, I grew up in New Orleans. There are all kinds of crazy there. But nothing like this. I had two broken ribs, a concussion, and being that I was underweight and barely holding on, I had a bit of a breakdown."

He wanted to tell her that a lesser woman would have fallen apart long before that, but he could see in her expression that she would never believe him. Instead, he gently pulled her out of the chair.

"What?"

He motioned to the bedroom. "Come on."

JOCELYN FOLLOWED Kai back to her bedroom, her nerves shot, emotionally wrung out. He closed the door behind her and led her to the bed. She hadn't been sure how he would take her story. It was one of the reasons she hadn't talked about it with anyone, her brothers, her sisters, her mother. No one other than Dr. Sawyer and the police. She didn't want to hear their questions. She knew her brothers especially were mad that she didn't tell them when it was going on. Worse, she knew she should have. She should have gone somewhere to report it. Even if no one believed her, she should have done it. The problem had been her pride. She'd worried what people would think of her. But here was Kai, and he had been willing to listen and not judge.

When Chris had shown up in Atlanta, the first thing he'd asked was why she didn't call him. Why had she let it get so bad?

It was as if he blamed her. And she knew without a doubt, he didn't. It was a reaction to the fear he had felt, but it had damaged something in her at the time. She had been so tired, so sick, so not wanting to live.

Kai stopped by the bed and turned her to face him. He smiled at her gently, lovingly, and she felt it all the way to her toes. How could a man be so gentle and sexy all at once? He undid the belt to her robe and slowly parted the fabric.

"Let me love you."

The words were simple, but they touched her heart, made it shiver with an emotion she didn't want to face. Not now, not after what she had just been through. But she knew that both of them needed this.

"Yes."

He smiled as if she had given him the world and bent his head to brush his lips over hers. It was a simple kiss, one that shouldn't have sent a lick of fire through her blood or made her knees weak. Like she had said to Cynthia, he made her melt. No man in her life had ever been able to do that with just a kiss.

He slipped her robe from her shoulders and then urged her to the bed. He pulled off his shorts and she couldn't help the desire that shifted through her. He was gorgeous. Lean, sculpted muscles, with various tattoos, the piercing, the solemn expression. And underneath, God, underneath was the best man she had ever known. He was so hot, sweet, kind...she was seriously losing herself to him fast.

"Lay back."

She did as he requested and he lifted her leg. With skill, he massaged her foot, his talented fingers moving over her arch. She moaned and closed her eyes. He gave her other foot the same treatment and then moved up her legs, caressing and kissing her skin. His tongue darted out every few kisses and then dipped into her belly button.

She laughed and he smiled at her. Then, slowly, easily, he moved closer. He took a nipple into his mouth as he took the other between his fingers and tugged on it. She felt it all the way to her pussy. Wet heat breathed through her blood. Leisurely, he built her up, with his tongue, his hands. It wasn't crazy, she thought as he slipped down her body, not like before. She felt his hot breath on her sex the moment before he touched her. She dug her fingers into the sheet as he drew her orgasm from her.

While she was still shivering, he grabbed a condom and slipped into her. When she went over the edge again, he went with her.

twelve

"You beat me here this morning," Cynthia said as she walked into the kitchen of the bakery. She was pale again, her hair a tangled mess, and she had dark circles under her eyes. "Wait, weren't you supposed to be off?"

Jocelyn smiled and shrugged. "I wanted to come in. Big question is how did you ditch my brother?"

Cynthia snorted. "It was a bad morning. I was up at three gagging, and hence...well you get the drift. He's so worn out. And stop laughing. I'm really starting to worry about him."

"Sorry. It's so much fun to hold over him."

Cynthia sighed as she tossed her purse into the office. "So tell me why you're here?"

"I told you, I just felt like coming in. I'm kind of worried about you." Even to her own ears it didn't sound truthful. It wasn't that she wasn't worried about Cynthia. She was a bit, but she knew morning sickness, along with the fatigue, were normal.

Cynthia crossed her arms beneath her breasts and tapped her foot. "Jocelyn."

She smiled. "I had to bring Kai back."

For a second, Cynthia's mouth opened and closed, twice, then she said, "It's about damned time. You've been here over a month. I never expected that boy to move that slow."

Jocelyn laughed. "There is nothing slow about Kai, except the good things."

"Oh really? That sounds so...naughty. I want some details."

Jocelyn shook her head. "No."

"Ah, come on." Cynthia was whining now and Jocelyn knew it was out of character. The hormones were really starting to get to her. "I've heard rumors about him of course. He has a bit of a reputation."

"If it is about the fact he has the stamina of ten men, then I would say it was pretty close to the truth."

"I'm happy for you, Jocelyn."

She glanced at her and recognized the gleam in Cynthia's eyes. She had seen it more than once in her mother's eyes through the years. "Don't go planning anything. Kai isn't the kind of guy who settles down, and I'm not sure if I can handle anything past taking things one day at a time."

Cynthia frowned. "I didn't say anything. But I have never seen him wait this long to ask a woman out."

"It wasn't like we haven't been on dates."

"Yeah, but well, Kai usually can talk a woman into bed on the first date."

Jocelyn shrugged. Lord knew that after that first turn around the island, he could have done. She had all but offered herself up to him that night, but he had held back. "I'm sure being linked through Chris and May made a difference."

She nodded as she grabbed the pink apron with the word Cynthia's splashed across the front of it. "I can see that, but still.

He's been kind of on his own since Keisha and he broke up. I just think he might be looking for something serious."

Panic set in first, along with a healthy dose of fear. "I'm not sure I can give that to him."

Cynthia looked up at Jocelyn's quiet admission. "Oh, honey." She walked over to her and pulled her into her arms. "You are right. You just have to take it one day at a time, but be sure not to forget that if there was a guy worth it, it would be Kai."

Jocelyn sighed. "That is probably the problem."

Cynthia pulled back and mischievous smile curved her lips. "So, there are rumors about certain piercings?"

Jocelyn laughed. "I don't kiss and tell."

Cynthia stuck out her tongue. "What fun is that?"

"Okay, only the nipple."

"Oh God, a nipple piercing. I wonder if Chris would go for it."

Jocelyn snorted. "I doubt that. He has a thing about the sight of blood. Just his own...although if I were you, I would think twice about having him in the delivery room. He might just pass out on you."

Cynthia laughed. "Leave your big brother alone. Poor man has had a bad time. He's lost about five pounds in the last two weeks."

"Only my brother would do something like that, butthead."

"I wish you hadn't called your brothers to tell them about the morning sickness."

"I think it's proper payback for telling my mother that I was sneaking out of my room at night."

Cynthia laughed. "I can see him doing that. But really, I'm

happy for you. You might not know where it's going, but it is nice to see you happy about a man."

KAI WALKED into Dupree's trying to figure just what he was going to say to Chris. He had cleared his schedule because he needed more information about the bastard who had hurt Jocelyn. He could have pushed her and she probably would have told him, but she had been so damned fragile after telling her story, he would have been a bastard to bother her for more info.

"Hey, Kai," Maryann, one of the full-time waitresses said to him. "May's not working today."

"Hey, I'm here to see Chris."

"Oh. Well, he's in the back doing something. I am not sure what. He's been spending a lot of time in his office."

Kai thanked her and headed to the back of the restaurant. He had liked Dupree's since it had opened and he had always been friendly with Chris. He was a good boss in a business that tended to have some real asses, and Kai was thankful that May had gotten a job here. He reached the office and frowned at the closed door. It wasn't like Chris to close his door. Kai knocked.

"Who is it?" Chris asked, his voice weak.

"Kai. Need to talk to you."

There was a pause and then Chris said, "Come in."

He opened the door and found Chris slumping down behind his desk. He looked like death warmed over.

"What's wrong with you?"

"Shut the door."

Kai did it and studied his sister's boss.

"This pregnancy is going to kill me. She better start keeping things down."

"Oh," Kai said, trying to hide a smile. "I forgot about that. Cynthia still having a bad time of it?"

Chris nodded. "Doc says everything is fine, but I don't know if I am going to be able to survive this."

Kai took a seat without being asked, but he figured Chris just didn't have it in him to be social.

"I came here to talk to you about Jocelyn."

Chris's eyes narrowed. "I thought you were going to leave her alone."

"Uh, I never said that exactly. I would have to be a fool, especially since your sister is a beautiful and intelligent woman."

Chris grunted as he sipped his water. "So, what did you want to ask me?"

"What happened to Greg?"

That had Chris pausing in drinking his water and studying Kai. "She told you about it?"

Kai nodded. It was still hard to keep his anger under control at the memory of her story. He had never felt so damned helpless in all his life. Even after his mother's death and the resulting mess it left the family in, he had never felt so impotent.

"She hasn't told me much. I mean, I got some from the police report."

He cocked his head and studied Chris. "Spying on your sister?"

Chris sat up a little straighter. "It is part of public record."

"Hey, don't get me wrong." He shrugged. "I would do the same for May, and being that they are both strong women, I won't tell her you did it. I have a feeling she would make your life a living hell for it."

"So what did you want to know about the bastard?"

"What do you mean?" Then he remembered his question. "Where is he?"

"Ah. Still in Georgia. Still waiting for trial." It was easy to see the disgust on Chris's face, to hear it in his voice.

"It's been months."

"Yeah, well, the courts are backed up, and since he is such a good citizen, he's out on bail."

"Fuck."

Chris nodded. "Exactly."

Anger and frustration had Kai popping up out of the seat and pacing. "You don't think there's a chance that he'd show up here, do you?"

"If he could, he would try. But she has a restraining order, and one of the best things to come out of this mess is that his restaurant business went to shit. His standing in the community sort of faltered. His wife just finished off his divorce and left him with nothing. Her lawyer was so ruthless, I was amazed she didn't end up getting alimony from him, even though she has all the money. So financially he can't make it over here. I doubt he has enough money to take a bus across town let alone a flight to Hawaii from Atlanta."

"You keep a close track on him?"

Chris nodded. "I have a friend who lives in Georgia. He's been keeping track of it. I protect what is mine."

Kai stopped and stared at Chris. "So do I."

Chris sighed. "So I guess you're serious. I'm not sure if she's ready."

Kai groaned in frustration. "Jesus, Dupree, I tried. But your sister has a one-track mind, and when she sets it to something there is no getting off that train. I can see how she graduated at the top of her class."

Chris smiled. "Yeah, it is a bit annoying. I guess there's nothing I can do about it."

"No. Knowing Jocelyn, if I broke it off because of you, she would first kick my ass, then yours."

Chris's eyes widened. "Holy shit, you know her well."

Kai shrugged. "She's an open book."

Chris shook his head. "No, especially not since her attack. She was so...closed off. Not like she wouldn't communicate, but she just doesn't share as much as she used to."

"Makes sense."

"Yeah."

"Well, you let me know if anything happens with that ass. I want to know right away if there is even the smallest chance that he could show up here."

"Are you going to protect my sister?"

"You forget that I started working on the docks at fifteen. I know how to protect what's mine. I also know how to make someone disappear."

"Duly noted."

"I got get going. I have some errands to run."

He had his hand on the doorknob when Chris stopped him.

"I'm not happy about this."

Kai looked over his shoulder at him, ready for a fight, but was relieved to see that Chris wasn't really angry.

"But as you said, Jocelyn doesn't do anything she doesn't want to. But by God, you hurt her and I'll hurt you right back."

"And I'd deserve it."

He left, knowing that he had just admitted to more than he

expected. And he was well and truly tangled up over a woman who would probably not be happy about it.

"You're brooding," Cynthia said as she sped around a slow moving truck. "Did something happen at work?"

He shook his head. "No. Kai came by."

She sighed and he could hear the disapproval in it. Cynthia hadn't been too happy with his behavior toward Kai since Jocelyn had arrived.

"Please tell me you were nicer to him than you have been lately?"

"I was." She made a disgusted sound. "Mostly."

"Christopher Michael Dupree—"

"Hey, don't three name me, woman. Damn, I laid off him because he wanted to talk about Greg."

She pursed her lips. "He was trying to pry information out of you?"

"How did someone as sweet as me get tangled up with such a nasty woman?" He shook his head and tsked. "No. She told him about it last night apparently."

"Huh."

"What?"

"Well, she didn't say anything to me about it. I mean, she told me about their date last night, but not that. And I find that more significant."

"Yeah, it made me think that this may be bigger than we expected."

"We?"

"Well, you know what I mean. They only just met."

"You wanted to whisk me away from Georgia after one night, sir."

He felt his cheeks heat. "Yeah, well, we're special."

She laughed, and as always his heart skipped a beat. She had the window open and the balmy afternoon air slipped through her locks. Even though she had lost a few pounds, her face glowed.

"I love you."

She smiled at him. "Good thing since I'm having your baby and we're getting married next month."

He sighed. "He seems to know her so well, and she seems like a stranger to me."

"Jocelyn? What do you mean?"

"She's so different."

"No, she isn't. You are thinking she is different and she is, from the idea you had of her in your head. But this woman isn't her. You still see her as a little girl."

"I do not."

"Yeah, or at least as a teenager. She's a wonderfully complex woman trying to get over a whole lot of crap. It is bad enough to go through something like that, but to have it public knowledge would be painful for a woman as proud as your sister. I'm not saying that she doesn't have scars. Any person who has suffered what she went through would. But she is a survivor in the truest sense of the word. She might be a little gun shy, but she is still that same woman underneath. She might do some things differently, like I know she is enjoying the little things more. But that doesn't change the fact that she is tough, or that she made it through something most people wouldn't."

"I never thought of it that way."

She smirked. "Yeah, I got that."

"Smart ass," he said, but it had no heat in it. "Don't you think it's odd that she told him?"

She shook her head. "She needed someone who would listen. Not judge and not try and fix it. You can't do that because you are the oldest and have been looking out for her for years. And this is someone who didn't know her before it happened. There would be no expectation of explaining her behavior during or after. Kai is one of the best sounding boards."

He remembered the way Kai had talked about her that morning. Chris understood the conviction in Kai's voice when he said he would protect her. Chris sighed. "He's a goner."

"Kai?"

"Yeah."

She frowned as she turned onto their street. "You make it sound like it is bad thing."

"It's just, I'm not sure Jocelyn is ready for it, and if she hurts him I think she might never forgive herself."

"Ahh, you're going to be such a good daddy."

She pulled into their parking space, parked the car and then leaned over to give him a kiss.

"Now, why don't I show you how much I love you?" she asked, her southern accent deepening.

"That sounds like a plan to me."

thirteen

Jocelyn greeted Kai at the door with a smile and the scent of tomatoes and garlic.

"You made me dinner?"

"I figured that I sort of owed you a decent dinner since we had only peanut butter sandwiches last night."

He smiled and stepped into her house before slipping his arm around her waist. "I missed you today."

Her eyes widened. It amazed him that she had no idea the effect she had on him. "You did?"

He wanted to tell her, right then, just what she did to him. He was just realizing that in a few short weeks of knowing her, she had tugged at his heart more than any other woman. But she would run the other direction screaming. So he settled for part of the truth.

"Yeah. I kept thinking wholly inappropriate thoughts while I was working."

Her lips curved. "Hmm, that sounds about like how I spent my day."

"How about we turn down the sauce and spend a little time discussing those inappropriate thoughts?"

"Hmm," was her only response as she took his ear lobe between her teeth. The little move sent a burst of heat through him. He was already keyed up just from driving here thinking about her.

He bent down at the waist and picked her up.

"Kai, put me down." She laughed when she said it.

"Naw."

"I'm too heavy."

He walked to her room. "Apparently not."

"Kai."

He stopped in front of her bedroom doorway and looked at her. "I know you're uncomfortable with it, but I like romance. I think you are a woman in need of it."

Her eyes softened. "You're a sweet man."

Just that look, and the way her southern whiskey voice drifted over the words, had his heart completely falling on the ground. At that moment, there was no turning back. What the hell had he been thinking? The moment he met her, he had been lost.

He said nothing, just bent his head to take her mouth in a sweet, hot kiss. Then he stepped into her room and laid her on the bed. It didn't take him long to get her naked. Soft, dark skin, long legs and those gorgeous eyes, he didn't think there would be a time he would ever get enough of her.

He slipped out of his clothes and joined her on the bed. As he kissed his way down her body, her moans grew and the sound of her pleasure filled the room.

THEY ATE their cold pasta in bed.

"I had no idea you could cook so well," he said around a mouthful.

She looked at him. "What do you mean? You've had my cookies."

He shot her a smile that did funny things to her heart. It was hard not to have those funny things happening with the man sitting in front of her. She had found out that Kai was not one bit embarrassed with his nudity. He sat on her bed, surrounded in Cynthia's feminine decor, and looked about as sexy and masculine as a man could. And bad. He was a naughty influence on her.

"Of course I've had your cookies. And then some."

She sighed and smacked him, but immediately started eating again. They had definitely worked up an appetite.

"Well, I had to take other courses, and when you first get into school you have to do other things. You have to have a well-rounded education."

"If you ever decide not to bake, you could make a fortune at cooking, that's for sure." He finished off his wine. "Do you want some more to drink?"

She shook her head. "I was going to get some water."

"I'll get you some." He walked out of her bedroom, again completely oblivious of his nudity. It was something different being waited on. Men had catered to her, but just the sweetness of grabbing her a water and letting her lounge around was something she'd never really had in her relationships. What did that say about the men she had allowed in her bed? Hell, what did it say about her that she chose those men?

A few moments later, she heard noise in her kitchen as Kai rummaged around for water. Then it struck her. She was sitting in her bed, wearing only a short robe, eating dinner with a naked man.

Dr. Sawyer would be so proud. And again, she had Kai to thank for it.

When he returned, he handed her water to her and then slipped back on the bed.

"So, you want to tell me about Mike?"

That surprised her. For some reason, she had thought he would have more questions about Greg at some point.

"We knew each other awhile before we started dating. Actually, I don't know if we knew each other, or knew of each other, if you know what I mean."

He flashed her another smile. "This is Oahu. I know exactly what you mean."

She laughed. "When you work within a field like mine, especially in a certain region of the country, everyone knows everyone else. We were actually fixed up by the sous chef at Greg's restaurant. Something Greg hadn't been too happy about. I guess I should have picked up on his strange behavior. He became very overprotective, but I assumed it was like my brothers. I know they love me, but sometimes it makes me want to shave them bald-headed."

He chuckled. "You sound like May."

"Of course I do. We have both dealt with idiot brothers." She sighed. "Mike and I hit it off right away. We had a lot in common."

"Both chefs, I can see that."

She nodded. "We also came from big families, had similar ideas on our careers. We'd even talked of opening a restaurant together. But when the issues with Greg started, he grew suspicious. Greg had that reputation with his students, and no matter what, Mike just wouldn't believe me."

"Stupid man."

"Why do you say that?" she asked

"You wouldn't cheat, Jocelyn. I told you that before." She grew uncomfortable with his earnest expression and tried to look away, but he stopped her by taking her chin in between his fingers. "You might have some faults, but you are honest."

She felt the hot press of tears against the back of her eyes. In all the months of horror of Greg, no one had believed her. Not one person she worked with, not even the man she had thought she loved.

"How do you know that?"

He slid his fingers over her jaw line. "One, because I know Chris. He's a good man and if he had some hand in your raising, I know it was done right. Two, because as I said, I know you."

She shook her head as an emotion she was afraid to name clogged up her throat. "No. You barely know me. You have no idea what a bitch I can be."

He leaned up and brushed his mouth over hers. "Yeah, I have an idea. I also know that you aren't the same person you used to be back then. You can't go through something like that and not change."

She sighed again, regret shifting over her as she tried to avoid eye contact. He held her jaw firmly and refused to let her look away.

"You see what you went through as something that shows a

weakness. That a stronger woman would have made it through with no problem. That's not right. Most people would have buckled long before you did."

She shook her head. "I'm not the same person."

The moment she said the words, she wanted to pull them back. They were too honest, too raw. And she had yet to admit it to anyone. Maybe even to herself. She had said the words enough times, but it wasn't until now that she realized how true it was.

"Don't."

"What?"

"Don't look like that. Don't ever be ashamed of anything you say to me. Not if you're being honest with me. Who gives a fuck who you were before?"

"I do."

He sighed. "I don't. I care who you are today. You might not be the same person to the world, but inside, where it counts, you are there. That strong core, that winner, she's still there. She might be regrouping a bit, getting by each day, but she's there. You're the same person. Your perspective is just different."

She shook her head as she felt tears roll down her cheeks. "My brothers want me to be who I was before. My family and friends. They don't like me like this."

He shook his head. "Oh, baby, you're wrong. What they want is to undo what happened."

She sniffed. "How do you know that?"

"Because of what happened to May. And going through what we did as kids." He took a quick drink. "After Mom died, we all changed. Dad, well he's always been Dad, but there was something different. He lost something we can't understand."

"You lost your mother."

He nodded. "Yeah, but it is different when someone loses a mate. It crushed him. I have never seen my father fall apart like that. It was scary but understandable. Aionas mate for life."

"Huh."

"And I would give anything to have my mother back, but there are good things that came out of it. May and I stayed close. It was at a time when I should have been moving away from her, getting older, but instead, it allowed us to be friends as well as brother and sister. It also made her one hell of a strong woman. And that is what I see in you. You were strong before and you're still strong. You just see yourself and the world differently." He smiled. "You're still Queen Jocelyn."

She felt her eyes widen. "Who told you that name?"

"Chris mentioned it a few times before."

He was sitting there, a quiet smile on his face, telling her she was a strong woman. He didn't blame her for her mistakes, wasn't waiting for her to fall apart. And he liked her just like she was.

She leaned forward and took his face into her hands and kissed him there. It was simple, in this room, in this moment. She felt such affection for a man because he said she was still the woman she was before. The kiss turned ravenous as she pushed him back on the bed. She heard a pasta bowl fall on the floor and she ignored it, ignored everything but this man. She lay on top of him as she slipped her tongue between his lips. She could taste the red wine, the pasta, the affection.

In that moment, she knew she was in major trouble. But she didn't give a damn. She sat, straddled him and pulled off her robe. She didn't know where it landed as she tossed it aside. His cock twitched against her pussy. She was already growing damp at the thought of having him inside of her, but she wanted something else, wanted to give him something.

He was watching her. His eyes were barely open, but Jocelyn could sense the hunger in them. Even in the dimly lit room. She kissed her way down his chest, slipping her tongue over his nipple ring, giving it a tug before she continued down. He was a delight of sinewy muscles and golden flesh. She couldn't get over some of the tattoos either. She had never been a woman into them, and she would never get them because she was a bit of a wuss when it came to needles, but on Kai, they added to his sensuality. She slipped off to the side of him as she reached his cock.

He was hard, waiting. She let her breath feather over the tip and smiled when it jerked. It was dark, filled with blood. She dragged her tongue over the top, enjoying the salty sweet taste of him. Even in this, it was different with Kai. Jocelyn had always been comfortable with her sexuality, but with Kai, there seemed to be no barriers. She took just the head of his penis into her mouth as she continued to swirl her tongue over it. Then she took him in her mouth. He groaned as he lifted his hips. Soon they were working in rhythm, as she started taking him farther and farther into her mouth.

"Fuck," he muttered the moment before he grabbed her hips and dragged her pussy over his mouth. His tongue slipped in right away, gliding over her clit again and again. He shook his head from side to side and then moaned against her clit. The vibrations moved over her flesh and pulled a moan from her. She slid her hand to his sac, squeezing him as he worked over her dripping sex, pulling her clit into his mouth. The scrape of his teeth had her coming, shivering with her release. But she would not stop. Even as she moaned, she widened her mouth to take all of him in. His cock bumped the back of her throat once, twice...

Then he came groaning her name as he arched against her.

Once he finished, he moved her off him and then pulled her up to him. He kissed her before she could even think. It was hot, sweet and just about everything in between. He pulled way and rested his head against hers.

"That was...there are no words."

She could hear his voice tremble slightly and she felt a surge of satisfaction. Kai was a sensual man, and if she could do that to him, well, that was pretty damn good.

"Stop looking so damned smug, woman."

She laughed and then hugged him. "Sorry. Hard not to after that."

She fell back against the pillows, Kai stretching out on top of her. He kissed her again and then looked down at her. Warmth filled his expression.

"Don't look at me like that. I am really messed up. I don't need—"

He kissed her and rolled over, pulling her with him. "You worry too much. Go to sleep."

She wanted to argue, but she was too exhausted to worry. She laid her head against his shoulder, took comfort in having his body next to hers and slipped into sleep.

THREE DAYS LATER, Jocelyn was still humming with satisfaction. Of course, that was easy to do because Kai had been at her house every night. They never really spoke of their commitment. Kai just started showing up when she closed up the bakery. Or she would wander down to the pier to wait for him to come back in. It was all kind of...comforting. Of course, today he was going to be late and he urged her to go home. With two crew members sick, he would have to work a double shift.

She had never really been a woman who expected a man to spend a lot of time with her. Even with Mike. She had always kept her career first and foremost in her life. Was that why it had all fallen apart when things went wrong? They had never really shared a lot of intimacies outside of the bedroom. In the few weeks she had known Kai, she had shared more of her past with him than she ever did with Mike. Why was that? Did she know she couldn't trust Mike, or was it because she didn't trust him that they fell apart? She knew without a doubt that she wouldn't have had the same problem with Kai.

That little fact scared the hell out of her. She wasn't ready to lose herself to a man. Maybe not ever. But of course, Kai didn't give a damn and just marched right into her life. She knew there were things he didn't tell her. She hadn't had the nerve to ask him more about Keisha. She wasn't sure if she could take him talking about another woman, especially the only one he had ever been serious about. Not right now, not when their relationship was so new.

"You got me some *mallasadas* this morning?"

She looked up to find the father of her preoccupation standing in front of her with a big smile.

"Mr. Aiona, how are you this morning?"

"Good. Enjoying the weather today."

"And yes, I have some *mallasadas* today. In fact I have one back here just for you."

Knowing that Kai's father loved the chocolate-pudding-filled *mallasadas*, she had saved one for him in particular. She grabbed his treat and then turned to him, "Want a cup of Kona with it?"

He smiled. "Only if I can get the prettiest girl in the room to share it with me."

"Why not? I have a break coming to me."

"Prettiest girl," Cynthia sniffed as she walked into the front of the store. "I can see that I'm being tossed aside for another woman."

Mr. Aiona laughed and gave Cynthia a hug. "You're abandoning me for married life with Chris. How are you feeling?"

"Pretty good. Morning sickness has definitely gotten better."

Jocelyn handed him his coffee and treat and said, "I was going to take a break."

Cynthia glanced around the shop. The customers had dwindled to just a few late morning tourists. "Sure. I'll try to see if I can handle this."

They picked a table outside to enjoy the morning sun and sweet breeze.

"Ah, that feels good, yeah? It has been a hot couple of days."

"Kai claims there's rain coming."

He nodded as he chewed on his *mallasada*. "Yeah, my boy knows the weather. You would think he was an old man with this knowledge."

She cocked her head and watched him.

"You have no problem with him over at my house every night?"

Mr. Aiona shrugged. "He's a grown man. He wasn't a virgin when you met him."

Jocelyn could feel her face heat at his plain talk.

"Oh, now, don't be embarrassed. My boy has always had some woman or other hanging around. But you...he's serious about you."

She nodded. "I know."

"Just make sure to be kind to my boy, so I don't have to stop coming here for my treats."

"You mean you'd find another shop that would give you this for free?"

He chuckled. "No. Definitely not as good. And I would come over, but I would have to frown at you."

She laughed. "I can see you doing that."

"You're liking it here."

A statement, one she had been thinking for several weeks. "It is hard to explain. Just...Hawaii is very soothing. It's like I am in tune with the lifestyle here, but I never thought it would be for me."

He nodded as he finished off his second *mallasada*. "Hawaii is a balm to the soul. I've known more than one person who came here and found themselves."

She shrugged. "It is an odd feeling. I know you know a little of what happened to me."

He nodded.

"I could never find a place I was comfortable. My house was too big, too...not what I needed. It wasn't that I was scared, exactly. It was like I didn't fit anymore. Here I do."

"Then that's all you need. Just know living on an island this small, there is always someone here if you need them. They'll leave you alone if you don't want to be bothered, but always be ready to lend a hand when asked."

She nodded. "I get that. I like it actually. I've met a few of my neighbors, know their names, their kids' names. In Atlanta, I didn't know one person who lived on my street. People never took the time to say hi. They were too busy with, well, whatever. And part of it was me. I was so focused on building my career I forgot to have a life."

He gave her a fatherly smile. "And now you have one."

She nodded, feeling the rightness of the statement and how much it meant to her. "Yeah. Now I have one."

AN HOUR LATER, she was closing up the shop when her cell phone rang. When she saw the familiar number, her heart jerked. What did Detective Morrison need with her?

"Hello."

"Jocelyn, how you doing?" the policeman asked. He had been the calm in the storm, with his easy Georgia-boy ways and his contempt for Greg. He had waded through the disbelievers and been a silent hero to keep her safe. He had believed her without question.

"Fine. I've been keeping myself busy."

"Probably not hard there in Hawaii. Is it as pretty as they say?"

Even with her nerves frayed, she looked out, down the street to the little patch of beach she could see. A nice soft wind still blew through the palm trees.

"Yeah. It is." She paused, then swallowed her fear and asked, "Why are you calling?"

The sigh she heard was filled with regret. "Greg cut a deal."

Greg's lawyer had been playing a game for months, and

175

with Greg's connections, she had always thought this might happen.

"What kind of a deal?"

"Community service, time served," he said, disgust dripping from his voice. "I threw a fit, of course."

She could barely hear the words as her brain went blank. Time served? For what he tried to do? The bastard had almost killed her, was intent on that, and they were going to let him walk around free.

"Jocelyn."

She shook her head. "Sorry. What?"

"I said I tried to resign from the unit—"

"No. You can't do that. We both knew this was a possibility when it came up. He has a record now. There isn't much he can do to get that off his record. Plus, he's ruined financially."

"Is that enough?"

She didn't know. "It will have to be."

fourteen

Kai arrived at Jocelyn's house, his body tired, but the drive had been worth it. He'd taken enough time to run back his house to shower. It had been a bitch of a day with unskilled fishermen and he'd gotten smacked more than once with a damned big mahi mahi. By the time he'd walked off his boat, he'd smelled like rotting fish.

He grabbed his overnight bag and walked up to the door. It was odd that in the last week he had started feeling more comfortable at Jocelyn's house than his own. It wasn't the house itself, that much he knew. He should be worried. He had never been one for sleeping over night after night. Here and there, no biggie, but there was a part of him that realized he was slowly moving in with Jocelyn.

He stopped in his tracks. Is that what he was doing? He glanced down at his bag and then at the door. She hadn't pushed, not once. Not like a lot of women. She just went happily along with the idea that he would be over and that they would plan their night together.

He was frowning as he walked up the steps. He could see

her through the screen door. She was sitting on the couch, sipping tea and reading over a cookbook. Something shifted in his chest. He had known he loved her. He probably hadn't had a chance since he'd met her. But this was something else entirely. He started to realize that she was more important to him than anything else.

Without knocking, another sign that he was practically living with her, he opened the door. She looked up and smiled. It didn't reach her eyes, but that might because she was tired. Dark circles marred the delicate skin beneath her eyes.

"Hey. How was your day?" she asked absentmindedly.

The simple question meant so much to him. He would have never thought himself a man who needed hearth and home, but to walk through the door after the bitch of a day he'd had, to a woman asking him that question, it felt right.

"Crappy. I got hit three times with a mahi mahi."

He set his bag down and walked to her. Taking her hand, he pulled her up off the couch, sat and then toppled her down on his lap. He kissed her, enjoying the warmth of her body, the taste of her on his lips.

When he pulled back, he said, "Hey."

She smiled again, this time it did reach her eyes. "Hey. Are mahi mahi big?"

"One weighed over one hundred and fifty pounds."

Her eyes widened. "Wow, I thought they were little fish."

Chuckling, he skimmed his hand over her bare thigh. "They are in the store."

"I guess so. Are you hungry? I had a sandwich."

"Don't worry. I can get it."

He picked her up and put her back down in the same spot, then headed into the kitchen. It was always neat as a pin, clean, sparkling. He knew part of it was because of her profession. May didn't cook in the restaurant, but she was a tiger about keeping the kitchen clean.

"How did your day go?" he asked as he stuck his head in the fridge to see what she had.

She didn't say anything at first, then, "Okay, your father came by to say hi."

Chuckling, he settled into making his dinner. "My father will always come in and say hi to you."

He thought he heard her sigh, but he might have been wrong. When he joined her in the living room, he settled beside her. "Do you want to do anything tonight? Both of us are off tomorrow."

She shook her head. "I have to go in. Someone came in with a rush order for a cake."

He pushed aside his irritation that they had lost their day together.

"But I should be done by ten in the morning. Then we have the whole day together."

"Am I that transparent?"

She shook her head, a smile curving her lips. "Naw. I was irritated too, but she paid Cynthia more for it, and I do enjoy doing the cakes."

"So nothing tonight."

She scooted closer. "Uh uh. I just like the idea of sitting here with you."

The small admission was an arrow straight to his heart. And so he smiled and enjoyed the feeling.

THE KNOCK at his office door pulled Kai away from his paperwork, but he wanted to curse when he saw Chris's face through the window. He motioned him in. He wasn't in the mood for another talk with Jocelyn's brother. But if there was one thing an Aiona understood, it was family.

"What can I do for you?" he asked Chris.

"When did it happen?" Every word came from behind clenched teeth.

Kai frowned. "What?"

"I wouldn't have known if I hadn't seen it online. Dammit, I can't believe she kept it from me, but I thought you would let me know."

He shook his head, still trying to figure out if he'd missed part of the conversation. "I have no freaking idea what you're talking about."

Chris stopped his pacing and stared at him. "He's getting out with time served."

For a second, he still had no idea about what Chris was referring to. Then it hit him like a punch to his throat. "Are you talking about Greg?"

He nodded.

"Can't be. Jocelyn didn't say a word."

"I read it online. He pleaded to attempted sexual assault, and because the judge knew him and knew it had been a horrible mistake on Greg's part, he is letting him off. Fucker." Sarcasm and anger dripped from every word. But Kai ignored it. His own anger was building, but not only against the system that needed to be fixed. No, there was a healthy dose for the woman who hadn't told him the news.

"When?"

Chris looked at him then. "What?"

"When the fuck did it happen?"

Chris must have realized she had kept it from him then. His face lost some of the anger. "From the date, early yesterday morning."

"Do you think she knows?"

Chris hesitated.

His anger swelled and normally he wouldn't let it bother him. Now though, he could barely control his need to hurt someone. "Don't treat me with fucking kid gloves. Tell me."

Chris nodded. "Yeah. Detective Morrison wouldn't have let her find out from another source. He would have called her yesterday."

She had been acting a little weird the night before. She had been tired, or so he had thought. Maybe it had been her worry over this. He stood up and walked out the office. Chris followed.

"Now don't get pissed at her for not telling you."

Kia stopped and turned to face him. He had always admired Chris, for what he was, for the way he treated Cynthia.

"What would you do if Cynthia did the same thing?" he asked.

Understanding moved over his features. "Okay, yeah, I would be pissed."

He turned around and started toward the front door again. "I'll have her call you after I yell at her."

"DAMMIT."

"Problem?" Cynthia asked.

Jocelyn shook her head and took off the decorative edge for the second time. "No. Just can't seem to get this right."

"You seem out of sorts."

Jocelyn jerked a shoulder, trying to hide the panic that was clawing at her stomach. She had been so close to taking her pills last night before Kai had gotten home. Once he'd arrived, she had felt his calming presence down to her toes. And he didn't even know it. She wasn't sure what scared her more. The fact that she might have needed her meds last night, or that Kai seemed to be her substitute.

"Hey, are you there?" Cynthia asked.

"Yeah. Just a little off today."

Cynthia frowned. "I knew I shouldn't have taken that order. This is your seventh day in a row working. You need to take tomorrow off."

Jocelyn shook her head. "No."

"Yes. No arguments. You're tired. I can see it. Of course, if I didn't know what was keeping you up at night, I'd worry."

Jocelyn felt her shoulders slump.

"What?"

"I had a bad night last night."

And now she had wished she had told Kai. She would have slept better if she had talked it over with him.

"No matter—"

"I need to talk with you, Jocelyn." Kai's quietly angry voice cut Cynthia's comment. She turned and found him glowering at her. Cynthia looked from one to the other and opened her mouth but Chris stepped in behind Kai.

"Let them have a moment."

He grabbed Cynthia and led her out of the room. When

they were alone, Jocelyn waited. The silence grew, the only noise coming from the front of the shop.

"What did you want?" she asked.

"Did they let the bastard off?"

Dammit, he knows. "Yeah. Or they will. I'm not sure."

"When did you find out?"

"Yesterday."

She couldn't tell what he was thinking by looking at his face. It unnerved her.

"That's why you were so upset last night."

"I wasn't upset last night."

"Yes, you were. There was something a little off, but then, how would I know. I apparently don't know you at all."

Agitation filled her. "What the hell does that mean?"

"The woman I thought I knew would have told me if something like this happened. Or I thought she would."

He said nothing else, but now she finally saw what he was feeling. Anger bled out of his eyes as he watched her as if waiting for her to lie.

"I'm used to dealing with things on my own."

He shook his head. "That's not going to fly. I thought we had something here. I thought we were building."

"I told you I was a mess. You apparently ignored that part of the conversation."

His upper lip curled in disgust. "Don't even try that shit with me. You kept it from me on purpose."

He thought she'd done it to hurt him. The accusation went unsaid. And, God help her, maybe she had. She had kept it from him on purpose, but she still wasn't sure why.

"Funny coming from a man who isn't ready to open up."

"What the hell does that mean?"

"Want to tell me what went on with Keisha?"

His expression blanked and his eyes turned colder. "That's in the past."

"Oh, Jesus, do you hear yourself?" Resentment she didn't know she had boiled up and spilled over into her panic. It made her voice harsher than she expected. "You, who wanted me to open up, tell you everything, doesn't want to tell me a thing about the one woman who broke his heart."

"That's bullshit."

"Really? Oh, that is rich." She barked out a laugh that sounded desperate and painful even to her own ears.

He clenched his jaw. "I said it was in the past. It has no effect on me now."

"If it didn't, you would have told me about it. At least I have been honest with you. You hold things back from me. Don't you think I know that Keisha stomped on your heart, used you and tossed you away? But for some reason, my pain is okay to go over, to share. Maybe this has more to do with the fact that you can't deal being with a woman who doesn't need you to save her."

The moment she said the words, she wanted to pull them back. But it was too late.

Pain shifted over his face first, then it dissolved into a remote expression she had never seen on him before.

"Well, don't worry. I'm out of the business of saving women."

And with that, he turned and stalked out of the kitchen. Cynthia returned a second later.

"Jocelyn?"

She was numb. Afraid to think, to feel. At the moment, she just didn't know what the hell to do. She concentrated on taking one breath, then another. He had left her. She knew she had used Keisha as an excuse to explain why she hadn't told him about the news of Greg's deal. But if there had been some truth to it, he wouldn't have gotten so angry.

"Chris." Cynthia's voice had turned panicky.

Chris came back in and Jocelyn felt warm arms surround her. "Come on, Jocey."

She almost allowed him to bundle her out of the kitchen, but she stopped at the door.

"No."

"What?" he asked.

She stepped away, straightened her shoulders and then looked from Cynthia to Chris. "No. I have a cake to do."

"Oh, Jocelyn, I can call the woman and tell her you couldn't do it," Cynthia said.

She shook her head. "No. I don't need to be taken care of."

"I think we need to call Dr. Sawyer."

She stepped away from her brother and raised her hand to his cheek. "I love you, but if you don't back off, I'll have to stab you with a fork."

His eyes widened. In the next instant, he stepped back.

"I'll have the damn cake done on time."

Then she would go home and fall apart.

fifteen

"I think you need to call Evan," Dee said as she walked into Micah's office. He smiled at his wife. She looked particularly interesting in her uniform tonight. Of course, he didn't know when she didn't look interesting in it. Or out of it for that matter.

"Stop looking at me like that, Micah. We don't have time. You need to call Evan."

"Why should I call my partner?" he asked.

She motioned toward the monitors. They showed his club Rough 'n Ready was starting to hop, but it also showed his business partner's brother-in-law drinking alone.

"It's his fifth whiskey in thirty minutes. I was about to cut him off. I know we have the one-drink max for the players, but we both know he isn't going into the rooms. And he's in one pissy mood, so I figured you might want to deal with him—or get Evan to. I'm assuming he had a fight with Jocelyn."

He was already dialing the number when Evan stepped into the office.

"Well, this is good timing," he said, rising from behind his desk.

"What?" Evan asked.

"You showing up. I was just calling you."

"Why?"

He nodded toward the monitors and Evan's expression relaxed. "I've been looking for him. He turned off his cell phone a while ago. May's been frantic."

Evan turned to go. "Need help?"

"Might. Boy grew up on the docks, and while I'm bigger, he's sneakier."

Micah followed him out the door. "I got your back."

KAI FELT them walking up behind him before he turned to look at them. He should have gone somewhere else, but he knew he'd picked Rough 'n Ready because he wouldn't pick a woman up here. How pathetic was he that he picked a place he could get drunk and not be tempted to cheat on the woman who had just shattered his heart.

"Hey there, son," Evan said, clamping a hand on Kai's shoulder. "I've been looking for you."

He cut him a look out of the corner of his eye and said nothing. He didn't care if it was sullen and immature, but he didn't feel the need to be particularly nice to anyone at the moment. Especially his brother-in-law who was seriously happy in love with May. Granted, most days he was happy for them, but tonight it was salt to his wounded pride.

"Sent out by my sister?" he asked with a snarl.

Evan smiled, but Kai could sense the brittleness to it. He squeezed Kai's shoulder as another hand came down on the other. He didn't need to look to know it was Micah.

"Why don't you come with us?" Micah asked, but he understood it wasn't a question. They would pick him up bodily to get him out of there.

"Fine."

He stopped by Dee. "Tattler."

Her eyes were soft. "I couldn't let you get that drunk. I could see that you would end up sick."

He smiled at her. "I should have stolen you from Micah."

"That I would have paid to see," Evan said as he urged him up the stairs. It took a while because Kai's feet didn't seem to want to work. By the time they dropped him on the couch, his head was spinning.

He closed his eyes to make sure he didn't barf. His stomach felt like a thousand mongooses were running around in it.

"Yeah, I found him. You were right. Well, he's lying on Micah's couch trying not to barf up the whiskey he drank."

"I am not." He cracked an eye open and saw Evan talking on the phone. "Who are you talking to?"

"Your sister."

He frowned. "No women."

Evan's lips twitched. "No problem. I'll take care of him."

"I'm not in the mood to deal with my sister."

"You and me both, but I held her off. I explained this is man stuff."

"Fucking A." He closed his eyes again. "Women aren't worth the problems they cause."

"Yeah, they are. It's a lot of shit, but they are definitely worth it."

He snorted and then had to fight another wave of nausea. "Fuck."

"You have such a way with words," Micah said.

He wanted to laugh, needed it, but it wouldn't come. Pain and anger still ebbed too close the surface. He wanted to hurt something, someone. He should have picked a fight so he didn't have to deal with it.

"Do you know what she did? Got the call, didn't call me. Dammit. Another woman, holding things back."

Comprehension and then pity moved over both Micah and Evan's faces. Shit. He didn't need this. But when he tried to pull himself off the couch, the room started spinning.

He fell back again.

"Okay, so she made a mistake. I have a feeling you've made more than one, and she hasn't called it quits. Of course, Jocelyn isn't stupid enough to call off a relationship because of small mistakes," Evan said.

He closed his eyes. "Didn't say she was. She just doesn't want a serious relationship."

"Huh." Evan said. "Really. That's odd because Chris thought you two were getting kind of serious."

He cracked one eye open and realized that Micah had left them alone. Evan was now sitting in the chair next to the couch.

"Well, he was wrong."

"Let me ask you a question."

"Can I stop you?" he asked.

"Did you tell her about Keisha?" Evan asked quietly

He didn't think he needed to answer that. He slammed his eyelids shut again.

Evan whistled and it pierced his head. "Oh, boy, you messed up."

"What the fuck does that mean?"

"You like to throw around the F word when you drink, don't ya?" Evan said, amusement threading his voice.

He gave his brother-in-law the finger, which just made Evan laugh.

"Let me put it to you this way, son. You accused her of not telling you something important, right?"

"Which she did not share with me, so I'm right. She found out about Greg's sentencing and didn't tell me. I had to find out from Chris."

"Okay. But she told you other things."

He frowned. "Yeah."

"Things she hasn't probably told anyone but her therapist. And did you open up and tell her about your mess? Of course you didn't. You're a man. As your sister likes to tell me, we were put on earth to mess things up. So what do you do now?"

An ache stabbed his heart. "It's over."

Evan sighed. "Come on. I'll take you to her. You can grovel."

He looked at his brother-in-law. "I don't wanna to go."

"Well, you have no choice. I love you both and you either fight it out, or break up. I do not want to deal with your sister if I don't try."

"You're a traitor to your sex." When that got no response, he said, "Puss."

"Yeah, you and me both. Come on."

Evan pulled him off the couch and then turned toward a back door to the office. Kai's eyes widened as they went past a big king-sized bed in a very elaborate bedroom, then out another door into the Hawaiian night.

"Damn, I never knew that was back there."

Evan shook his head and helped Kai down the stairs. "Son, I have a feeling there are a lot of things you don't know about. And knowing Jocelyn the way I do, you're about to learn a thing or two."

JOCELYN DRAGGED herself into the kitchen and started a kettle to brew some tea. She had been a mess since she'd arrived home. She didn't like to admit that she'd messed up, but she had, a little bit. But she knew there was part of her that understood why she had done it. Even before talking to Dr. Sawyer, she had known that Kai had held things back from her. Hadn't she thought just that earlier that day?

With a sigh, she opened the cupboard but paused when she heard a car door. It was too close to be a neighbor's car.

"I said I don't wanna be here."

That was Kai. Or at least it sounded like Kai. A very drunk Kai. On the way to the door she saw Evan tugging Kai out of his truck.

"I don't care. I said you're staying here."

With amazing ease, Evan stood Kai against the truck and then leaned down to pick him up over his shoulder. He walked with purpose to the front of her house. What the hell happened?

She went to the door and opened it just as Evan walked up the stairs.

"Well, there you are. Cute as a bug," Evan said.

"What the hell are you doing here?"

"I said I don't want to be here," Kai said, then he burped.

"Shut up," Evan said good-naturedly as he continued toward her. She had no choice but to let him through the door.

Kai lifted his head, his lips in a snarl. When he saw her, it dissolved into a drunken smile. "Hey, Jocelyn. Your eyes are really green tonight."

Evan chuckled as he continued on to her bedroom. She didn't follow them, but heard Evan murmur something to Kai and then he came back out.

"Lord, he weighs a ton."

The tea pot went off and she hurried to the kitchen. "Why the hell are you bringing him to me?"

He shrugged. "You caused it. I figured you should have to clean up after him."

She poured the steaming water over her tea. "And just what the hell do you mean by that?"

"Are you going to offer me any?"

"No."

"Mean woman."

"Evan."

"Oh, well, you broke his heart."

Pain stabbed at her chest and she tried to regain her composure before Evan saw it. She was unsuccessful.

"Hey, don't get too upset. I know you're both hurting." He took her mug and set it on the counter. Like the big brother he had always played in her life, he pulled her into his arms and rocked her. "I just couldn't leave him in Rough 'n Ready or he would have had a fight. And I figured it was best to bring him here instead of bail him out of jail."

Her heart sank. He had already been out looking for another woman. Dammit. So she messed up, but was that any reason to abandon her? She had thought he might blow off some steam, but to run out the first night and look for a woman?

Evan pulled back and said, "And I know how your head is working. No, he wasn't there for women. He never went there except when Keisha was there working as a waitress. He was there probably to make sure he didn't do something stupid. He doesn't play, and you have to know that."

She nodded.

"Now, make him cry and take pictures. I would appreciate it if you would post them on Facebook. He deserves it."

She sniffed. "How do you know?"

Evan chuckled. "As my lovely wife told me earlier, it is always the man's fault. But be gentle. He is head over heels in love with you, or at least he smells that way. Who knew the boy could drink that much whiskey?"

He kissed her nose then she walked him to the door.

"May is relieved he's here. I was sent out as the search party when he turned off his cell phone."

She nodded. "Thanks, I think. Although I'm not sure what to do with him."

"Let him sleep it off. He'll pay enough in the morning. Night, sugar."

He kissed her cheek then jogged down the stairs. A moment later, she watched his taillights disappear into the night. She closed the door and locked it, then picked up her tea on the way back to her room. For a long time, she stood by the doorway and looked at him. He was a mess, his shirt halfway up his torso, exposing that lean washboard stomach. He had his arms flung wide as if calling a touchdown. She wandered closer and then squatted beside his side of the bed.

His eyes popped open. "Hey, Jocelyn. Come on to bed." The tone of his voice told her that he had other things on his mind than sleeping.

"Not sure that's a good idea."

He frowned as his eyes drifted closed. "But I love you, you crazy woman." Then he started snoring.

It would have been comical if she hadn't felt her heart almost fall out of her chest onto the floor. Did he really mean it? There were times when he looked at her that she thought he might. But it could be the alcohol talking. Men said really stupid things when they were drinking. Hell, people did. Still, there were times when he pulled her close and the look in his eyes told her he felt at least something more than lust.

The memory of his accusations that afternoon came back to her. He had been in pain. They both had, but she could feel his as strongly as hers. He did love her. She kept seeing the pain in his eyes as he asked her about Greg. But it wasn't just that. The way he had loved her after she told him about Greg should have told her then.

Still, the man had another think coming if he thought he could say he loved her and she would forget it all.

Because this one time in her life, Queen Jocelyn wanted it all. And dammit, Kai Aiona was just going to have to deliver.

SOMEONE WAS TRYING to break his head open. Or at least it felt that way to Kai. He tried to open his eyes and should have known better. The sun had been hot on his face and now it seared his eyeballs.

"Fuck."

"That's a good way to put it," Jocelyn said.

Fuck. He was at Jocelyn's house. How did that happen?

"You might want to get up because considering how much whiskey your brother-in-law claimed you drank, you probably need to use the bathroom."

With that she left him blessedly alone. It took him some time to be able to open his eyes again. When he could, he slowly rose to sit up in bed. His stomach threatened to lose the contents and he closed his eyes. He heard her soft footsteps as she walked toward him. She grabbed his hand, placed something cool in it. He opened his eyes and found a glass of clear, fizzing liquid.

"Drink it. If you are going to lose it, you'll clean it up if it ends up in my bed."

Again, she left without waiting for an answer. It took him longer to drink down the cure than he expected, but he kept it down. Twenty minutes later, he walked into the kitchen to the smell of food. He'd showered and it had cleared his mind. He had a lot of apologizing to do for his behavior yesterday.

She apparently hadn't heard him, so he felt free to watch her as she puttered around the kitchen. God, he had been an ass last night. He didn't know what he had said to her, but he hoped he didn't say anything he would regret. It was all fuzzy, but he remembered Evan dragging him out of the club. He also had a vague memory of Evan carrying him into the house.

She turned and her mouth opened as she gasped. "Don't sneak up on me."

He walked to her then, took the plate of food and placed it

on the kitchen counter. Taking her face into his hands, he leaned closer and kissed her. Long, slow, sweet.

He pulled back, but held onto her face. "I'm sorry."

"You didn't do anything—"

"For yesterday. For blaming you for something I did."

She frowned at that.

"I should have told you about Keisha. Should have told you everything, but I hadn't dealt with it."

And he had allowed the ignorant actions of his old high school sweetheart to make him almost lose this woman. The one he wanted forever.

"I want to tell you about her, about why I messed up."

She sighed. "I would like that."

"But not right at the moment. First, I need coffee. And I need to grovel. Or I think that Evan said I did."

She picked up a mug and handed it to him. "Food's for you."

She wandered out to the little lanai and he joined her there a few minutes later.

"Thank you."

She glanced at him, then back to the view. "What for?"

"First, for taking me in last night. Not sure that I would have gotten any care at home. Probably would have gotten yelled at."

"Why is that?"

"I think my father would kill me if I messed things up with you."

She smiled. "Yeah, I got that feeling when he called looking for you last night."

Damn, it was like he was a teenager again, his father looking for him past curfew. "Sorry about that."

She shook her head and looked at him. "'I understand. I was worried when I couldn't reach you, but I thought you might be ignoring me."

He heard the catch in her voice and felt like a bastard. She looked away.

"Jocelyn, I'm sorry."

She nodded.

"No. I am sorry." He took her hand and tugged on it until she looked at him. "I was an ass. I expected everything from you, but I wasn't willing to share. I should have. There wasn't much I could tell you other than Keisha used me. I thought I was okay with it until she packed up and left. And I knew if I had realized my feelings earlier, she might have not left and took off with that bastard."

"You feel guilty. It's not your fault."

He shook his head. "Not all my fault. But partially. I should have realized. I'm not sure if we would have lasted. I doubt it. But I would have liked to have tried."

"Why do you think you two wouldn't last?" she asked.

He looked at her hand as he played with her fingers, then glanced back up at her face. "Because I realize I was waiting for you."

Tears filled her eyes. "Oh, Kai."

"I know that it sounds stupid."

"It doesn't sound stupid at all."

"I wasn't always truthful with Keisha. Not that I lied or cheated, but I kept it light because I thought she wanted it that way. Maybe she didn't, I'm not sure. But I didn't take the chance. I just didn't want to do that with you. I didn't want to lose you."

She slipped her fingers in between his. "I want to explain to you why I didn't tell you about Greg."

She drew in a breath and he knew she was trying to pull herself together.

"You don't have to."

"No. I do. I was trying to deal with it, trying to figure out just how to cope."

He cocked his head and studied her as she looked out over the small backyard again. He heard something in her voice.

"I was on medication before I came here. All kinds of medication. Well, two types. Mostly to help with the anxiety."

"I know and it's understandable. Anyone who had been through what you had been through would need something."

She snorted, but he heard the pain and embarrassment.

"You're a fantastic woman, but you're not superwoman."

She cast him a look that would have had another man running away. But he wouldn't. He wanted her too badly and she needed to know the truth.

"You're not perfect, Jocelyn."

Frowning she asked, "What do you mean by that?"

"You're high maintenance."

"I am not."

"You are too. You want things a certain way. There's a reason your nickname was Queen Jocelyn. And I am sure you liked the name. It fits you."

"Oh, really?"

He nodded. "Yeah, babe. You won't let me clean the kitchen, and more than likely, you've reorganized Cynthia's kitchen at work."

Her expression blanked as she pulled her hand from his and

then crossed her arms. "If I am such a pain, why do you even want me?"

He shook his head. "Damned if I know. Probably the masochist in me."

Now her eyes narrowed and lit with green fire. She opened her mouth and he started laughing.

"God, you should see yourself." He plucked her out of her chair and settled her on his lap. "I love you. Everything. The good and the bad. I don't expect you to be perfect. I just want you to be Jocelyn."

Her expression softened then. "You told me you loved me last night."

He felt his face flush and wondered what other embarrassing things he had said to her.

"Then you called me a crazy woman."

He laughed. "And do you have something to stay in return?"

Her lips curved and her eyes sparkled with devious humor. "Thank you?"

"Jocelyn—"

"I love you. And just like me, you're not perfect. Although, I do believe I am closer to perfect than you are."

He gave her a kiss. "You definitely are. So you're hanging around?"

"Yeah. I was wondering...since you had so much stuff here already, well, clothes, did you want to move in with me."

His heart constricted when he heard the uncertainty in her voice. Even after a declaration of love, she wondered. He would definitely use the rest of their lives to prove that he was around to stay.

"Yeah." He swallowed the lump that had risen in his throat.

"Yeah, I would like that a lot. Although, we will need something bigger and closer to Honolulu in the future."

She kissed him, sweet, long, wet. "I love you, Kai."

Her whisper reached past his heart, right down to his soul.

"I love you too."

And they sat there, watching the day come alive around them in the glow that they had found what they needed.

epilogue

Two months later

K ai was helping a customer onto his boat when he caught
sight of Chris. Worry hit him first as he stepped out of
his boat and onto the dock. He was dressed in his work clothes,
a white shirt and dark pants, so he had just come from work.

"Chris, is everything okay?"

Chris' eyebrows rose up. "Whoa, cool your jets. Everything's fine."

Relief filtered through Kai, and he realized how stupid he
had been. If there was an emergency, Chris would have called.
And now he looked like an idiot.

"Don't worry, bra. I understand."

There was only kindness in Chris' eyes and Kai nodded.

"Once they get a hold of you, even a little worry can leave
you spinning, right?"

Kai nodded, pulling in a deep breath.

"Then why are you here?"

He smiled and rocked back on his heels. "Here's your coat, what's your hurry?"

He blew out a breath. "Sorry. I just thought you were working today. "

"I am. I just wanted to stop by since you are moving in with Jocelyn."

Kai tried his best not to take offense. Chris had definitely accepted that Jocelyn and Kai were a couple. There was still a vibe Kai got from the other man. Chris was keeping a close eye on him.

He nodded. "As of last night."

"Listen, I was kind of an ass when you first showed up."

"Kind of?"

He flashed Kai a smile as he stepped out of the way of some of Kai's patrons. "Yeah. You get it, right?"

He did. He would do anything to protect his siblings. If they had been through what Jocelyn had been through? Yeah. He definitely understood.

"I do."

"Good."

Then he stood there staring at Kai. A long moment of silence started to turn awkward as both of them continued staring at each other.

"Anything else?"

"No. I just wanted to clear the air. "

"Like I said, I get you. I will do everything in my power to always be there for her."

"Fair enough."

"Kai!"

He looked back over his shoulder at Vince.

Looking back at Chris, he noticed the other man had turned a little ashen.

"I thought the morning sickness was over."

"Don't. I..." He swallowed. "Listen, I told Cynthia I was fine. She was feeling guilty, and," another swallow, "she doesn't need any more stress."

"No problem, bra. I get it. So, I guess no boat ride today?"

Chris gave him the finger as he returned to the parking lot. With a smile on his face, Kai hurried back to his boat. He had a day with tourists and a night planned with the love of his life.

"Has my brother finally admitted that he still has morning sickness?"

Cynthia chuckled. "No. Silly man thinks he has me fooled."

"Mama thinks it's hilarious."

"So, what do you think about the new job?" Cynthia asked.

Jocelyn glanced over at her. She was hitting her second trimester and glowing with her pregnancy. "I think the decision is yours."

Cynthia shook her head as she slid her hand over her stomach. Jocelyn hid a smile. Her brother's girlfriend wasn't really showing at all, but Cynthia's hand seemed to gravitate to her stomach. It was adorable, and Jocelyn was jealous of another woman's pregnancy for the first time ever.

It was a bright Sunday afternoon, and she and Cynthia spent it at home. Cynthia had finally gotten over the worst of her morning sickness, and she had suggested that they watch TV and vegetate on the couch since Chris was at work.

"No, this is your decision. You know I can't do the decorating, and while I can bake a cake, it will be nothing compared to yours. And it would put you under pressure because this is a big undertaking. They want a regular wedding cake, a groom's cake, and cupcakes. I can handle that last part, but you must do the other two."

"Are you sure it was Jakob Wulf, the actor, who requested a cake?"

Cynthia nodded. "Well, his people did. Apparently, one of his friends is getting married, and Jakob had one of your cakes when he was in Atlanta filming something."

"*Blank Space.* It was that thriller about the female serial killer. We handled the wrap party."

She had been star-struck when the English actor had complimented her over the cake she had crafted.

"He said something about blood spurting."

Jocelyn nodded. "When they cut into the cake."

"Well, he doesn't want that, and it isn't for him. It's for his best friend who lives here. Keanu Kingston. Runs Kingston Surfing."

"And he's the one getting married?"

"Yeah, this year. Apparently, Jakob kept going on and on about that cake, so when that reporter did that spread on you, Keanu called his friend."

A month ago, the biggest newspaper on the island featured Cynthia's Bakery, and mainly Jocelyn was the new cake baker. The orders poured in so fast they could barely keep up with the phone calls.

"Why didn't this Keanu Kingston just call?"

"He did. Or rather, the wedding planner did. We were already booked up at that point."

"But we're going to now?"

Cynthia nodded. "Having the best friend of a movie star as a client...not bad. Plus, the Kingstons have a lot of clout here on the islands. But I didn't want to say yes unless you felt you could do it."

Jocelyn looked over the notes that Cynthia had jotted down. The bride wanted a four-tier cake and a massive groom's cake with a surfing theme.

"I'll warn you. When I talked to Tracey, she said the bride was a bit of a pain in the ass."

Jocelyn looked up. "Tracy?"

"The wedding consultant. She handles Aloha Weddings, the biggest wedding planner business on the island."

Cynthia's gentle tone told Jocelyn that she would turn them down if the pressure was too much.

"That would be good."

The frisson of excitement was already spreading through her blood. She wanted to do this. She even had some fantastic ideas already, thanks to the detailed request.

"That's from the groom's sister."

Jocelyn looked up at her. "What?"

"The groom's sister has been handling a lot of stuff, and according to Tracey, she's shielded people. Her soon-to-be sister-in-law sounds like a real bitch."

Jocelyn smiled.

"What?"

"It's funny when you cuss. You sound like Scarlett O'Hara."

Cynthia rolled her eyes. "So, what do you think?"

"I think we should do it. It will be good exposure, and I even have a few ideas for the theme and flavors."

"Yay!" Cynthia said, jumping off the couch. "We have so much to plan."

She returned to the living room with a notebook and pen.

"Ready to plan for the next few months, which will be insane?"

She thought about it, about her new life here in Hawaii with her new friends and her new man.

"You're damned right. I'm ready."

KAI SMILED as he said goodbye to the last of the tourists for the day. The last couple of months had been busy, busier than he had ever been before. They were turning people away regularly.

Everyone else was gone because Jocelyn was coming to meet him. They'd planned to take the boat out for a sunset dinner together. They both had been busy the last few weeks, and they made it a point to plan this nighttime excursion since both of them were off tomorrow.

He busied himself with policing the boat cleaning up some trash, and before he knew it, the sound of sandals against the dock caught his attention. His entire body reacted. He had a feeling that he would always have this reaction.

"You are a sight for sore eyes, *Ipo*."

She took his hand and let him help her down. "You know it gets me all hot when you call me sweetheart in Hawaiian."

He pulled their joined hands up to his mouth, brushing his mouth over her fingers. "Then I will do it much more often."

He glanced down at her other hand and noticed the basket.

"You are full of surprises."

"Well, we couldn't go out on a dinner date without something to eat."

He smiled. "Then we should get going."

She nodded, and he got the boat ready to head out. They went out to one of his favorite places to watch the sunset. Once he dropped anchor, he joined Jocelyn at the table on the ship's deck. The air was sweet and crisp, the view was stunning, and it was perfect to share with his woman.

As they enjoyed their simple meal, Kai couldn't think of a better way to end his Sunday.

He looked at Jocelyn. "I love you."

She smiled. "I know. I am pretty lovable."

He laughed.

"I love you too, Kai."

And with the water lapping against the boat and sun sinking below the horizon, Kai knew life just didn't get better than this.

The End

THANK you so much for reading A Little Harmless Addiction.

If you loved it, please make sure to leave a review or rating at your favorite online site.

Coming Next in the Harmless World: Rough Submission!

Detective Rome Carino has his hands full with a killer bent on punishing women who frequent the club, especially when he FBI Agent Maria Callahan

rough submission excerpt

ROUGH SUBMISSION

For a tough as nails Dom hunting a sadistic serial killer is nothing compared to losing his heart.

Rome Carino isn't the kind of man anyone would call soft-hearted, but that's okay. It's one of the things that make him good at my job as a detective with Honolulu Police Department. He will need all his skills as sharp as possible while I hunt a killer targeting the popular club Rough 'n Ready. Keeping his mind on his work is usually not a problem, but then that was before the FBI Agent **Maria Callahan** was assigned to the case.

Maria has always lived in her Legendary father's shadow. She's spent her entire life trying to live up to his high standards. She's never been able to keep her mind on her work until she met Rome. The sexy detective scrambles her pulse and her brain, but she's never been the kind of woman to throw herself at a man. Besides, she and Rome have a job to do. The only problem is Rome refuses.

Rome knows it's a good plan, but an irrational protectiveness has taken hold of him. The only way he will agree to the scheme is to act as her boyfriend, which puts her up close and personal with Maria. From the start, the line between real and fake blur, and soon both of them start to fall. it is irrational.

But before they can deal with their feelings, the killer they're hunting turns his sights on Rome, and the one person he cares about: Maria.

» **WARNING: The following book contains: A man who thinks he can do no wrong, a woman who is about to teach him he can, palm trees, a trip or two to Rough 'n Ready, a flirty Aussie with questionable motives, old friends, and a new enemy. Yeah, it might be a Harmless World book, but Addicts know it's anything but.**

Rome cursed when the rain started to pound the top of his car. It figured he would get a call for a dead girl and it would rain like this. That's the way his luck had been going the last few months. Only with hurricanes did they get this wet in Honolulu. What little forensic evidence they could have found was probably being washed away right now. He hoped that CID got there early enough to collect samples. He turned down Kuhio Street and headed to the scene. He had an itch at the base of his neck that told him this fourth girl in three months was connected to the other three. In all his life, he had never believed in coincidences, and he wasn't about to start. What that meant for Rough 'n Ready was not something he wanted to contemplate right now. He would deal with that later.

He parked his car and sighed. There was very little media on the islands, but they all seemed to show up at his crime scenes lately. A small group had gathered at the front of the alley. Lord only knew how they discovered the scene, but on Oahu, it was like one big family. Everyone knew everyone else, and there was just no way to stop people from finding out.

He stepped out of the vehicle, grabbing a hat before shutting the door. He turned up his jacket collar against the rain. Lord, it was cold. Rome had gone soft. For a kid who grew up in Seattle, this would be nothing. Now, after just a few years, seventy degree weather had him shivering.

He shook those thoughts away and made his way to the scene. Several reporters tried to get a comment from him, but he ignored them as he pushed his way through the crowd. He was thankful to see the CID officers already working the scene.

He glanced down and saw the girl. And, like the others before, he knew her.

A rookie cop ran up, excitement and fear in his voice when he spoke. "Her name is Lisa Fender. Here's her wallet."

Rome accepted it and was thankful the young officer seemed to be holding it together. "Who called it in?"

"Tourist. He's over there," he motioned with his head. "Name's Matt Young."

Rome followed the direction of the officer's nod and found a young man standing, his face expressionless as he watched the scene in front of him. Truthfully, from what Rome could tell, the witness wasn't really watching anything. He was staring into nothing, as if in a daze. Shock probably.

After thanking the kid, he headed over to the witness. "Mr. Young?"

For a moment, Young didn't say anything. Rome started worrying the kid had gone over the edge and might need medical care. But, in that next moment, Young shook himself and seemed to focus on Rome. "Huh?"

"I'm sorry to bother you, but I'm Detective Carino. I was wondering if you could tell me what you saw."

Mr. Young swallowed, his Adam's apple bobbing as he nodded. Damn, he was young. In that instant, Rome felt ten years older than his thirty-five years. There was a good chance Young wasn't even old enough to drink.

The kid wiped his mouth on the sleeve of his shirt. "I was walking down here. Got left at a club by my buddy."

"He left you at a bar? Why?"

He sighed. "He hooked up."

Rome nodded, understanding the timeless ritual of young men. Being left behind at a bar for a hot woman wasn't that bad of a thing. As he studied the man, Rome recognized the buzz cut.

Fuck. Rome wasn't in the mood to deal with the military. "What service?"

The kid's eyes widened. "I have n-no idea—"

"Cut the shit. You're military."

He swallowed again, then his shoulders sagged. "Yeah. Army."

"And let me guess, too young to be in the club you were in? Not to mention, it's off limits to military."

He swallowed again. "Yeah."

"I don't give a shit about that. What I care about is that woman lying dead on the ground."

The kid started breathing through his mouth, and Rome should have seen it coming. As it was, he barely missed getting the kid's vomit on him. Rome jumped back with a curse as the private emptied his stomach contents on the street.

"Fuck."

"You said a mouthful, Carino."

Rome turned and found his partner of just over a year walking up behind him. Jackson Daniels—who everyone called Jack Daniels just to piss him off—was officially his partner for the next three days. The paperwork was already filed, and Jack would be gone before the month was out.

"What are you doing here?" Rome asked.

He shrugged. "I got the call, too. Thought I would stop by."

His knowing look told Rome that his partner thought the same thing he did. "You can't finish out the investigation."

"Yeah, but I can take the rest of the kid's statement. Why don't you get over there with the body, talk to the geeks?"

Rome wanted to correct Jack's use of the name, but decided to ignore it. Jack was the kind of cop that would use the science CID gave them, but hated it just the same. It was one of the things that had always been a bone of contention between the two of them. Thank God Jack wasn't Rome's responsibility anymore.

"Sure. I got up to the part where he and his other underage buddy parted ways because of a hot girl."

Jack shot him a grin. "Hey, it happens."

Rome chuckled as he turned and worked his way toward the scene. He could just imagine what it had been like for a woman to walk down the alley. Lights illuminated the dark corners now, but it would have been gloomy, dank...not to mention the smell of rotting food and booze. No one, whether woman or man, would walk down this alley without a purpose in mind. And definitely not alone.

The first person to notice him was Tim Takewodo, a first-rate detective with the CSI. He had been the lead on all the investigations so far, and having him there made Carino feel somewhat better.

"Hey, Carino. Glad to see that you got the call."

He nodded. "What ya have?"

Tim's smile faded. "Raped. Beaten, strangled. Coroner will have to give us the exact way she died. Panties are missing again."

He shot Tim a look.

"Yeah, I'm guessing manual strangulation like the others, and I'm sure he also used a scarf. I'm sure we will find the same fibers on her. I take it you know her?"

He looked back down at the young woman. He had seen her at Rough 'n Ready once or twice. "She looks a little familiar. I didn't recognize the name, but since I started working homicide, I haven't had as much time over at Rough 'n Ready."

It was a half-truth. Rome was avoiding his friends. He'd had to distance himself from his friends to make sure there were no questions later. He had learned a long time ago to never take anything for granted. He knew in his gut that Micah and Evan had nothing to do with this, but he needed that separation to make sure they didn't get tangled up in the investigation.

"They have a lot of new members, and with the new club opening on the other side of the island, they had to hire new people. She might be one of the newbies."

Tim sighed. "I'd lay odds. And this makes the fourth one."

Rome nodded, knowing it would prick the interest of the

FBI. Dammit, he wasn't in the mood to deal with the feds. They would definitely come in and take over the case. "Find anything new?"

"Nope. Again, we can't be sure she was raped until there's a kit done."

Rome wanted to argue. Because the first three women had been regulars or worked at Rough 'n Ready, people thought they were into any kind of rough sex. Because a person was into BDSM didn't mean they would do something stupid. In fact, a lot of times, people in the life were smarter than most about that part of their life. Anyone with any sense wouldn't end up having sex in an alley of Kuhio Street. It was one of the rougher parts of Honolulu. Why leave the nice, warm environment of Rough 'n Ready and wander into a backstreet that would leave them vulnerable? Didn't make sense, but it was his job to make it make sense.

Rome glanced around. "Have you seen a car nearby that might be hers?"

"They did a search. Haven't found it, but that doesn't mean anything. You know if she was club hopping..."

She could have parked anywhere in the area. Tonight's weather aside, a person could probably bet on warm enough weather to make it from here to at least a bus stop.

"Thanks, Tim."

He turned and saw the coroner had arrived. The sooner they got the poor woman out of here, the better. And then maybe they could find the bastard who did it.

Rome looked out over the crowd, wondering where the son of a bitch was hiding.

Maria Callahan pretended to be reading something on her computer as she waited. Still, she couldn't stop her toe from tapping. She wasn't very good at waiting. It was one of the few lessons her father had failed to teach her. It was hard to be patient when something that could make or break your career was being decided.

She knew this was The Dom. Maria grimaced. That name irritated her, but reporters thought it was catchy. Damn reporters were making it damned hard to catch him. These new killings in Hawaii were him. She could feel it to her bones. Besides that, she had done enough research to know it was him. Her plan could work, and for once, she had worked up the nerve to approach her supervisor about it. It was unorthodox, but it could work.

"Callahan!" Agent Smith bellowed. "Get in here."

It took every bit of her control not to jump and run.

Don't even let them see you sweat. Make them think they can't rattle you. Falling apart is for later.

Drawing in a deep breath, she slowly stood and walked to her supervisor's office. She shut the door.

His head was bent, showing her the bald spot none of them were allowed to mention. He had put on a few pounds in the last several years, but he was still in good shape. He signed a form then looked up at her. His face was expressionless. She still could not tell what her father's old partner was thinking. Then he smiled.

"It's a go. I talked to the HPD captain. He agreed we need to be there. He wants you working with his man."

She could barely pay attention for a few seconds. For the first time, she was going to head an investigation.

"Callahan." Smith sounded worried. She realized he had said her name several times. She gave herself a mental shake and focused her attention on her boss.

"Sorry," she said, then cleared her throat. "The detective? He's been checked out."

Smith nodded. "He's been on the island for the last eighteen months, except for one trip to Seattle for the weekend. Sister graduated from college. He didn't leave the area. So he's clean. Apparently he's pretty sharp, so try to play nice."

He said it sarcastically, and she tried not to wince. She didn't like the fact that she would be walking into a local department and taking over their investigation. It had to be done sometimes, but the behavior of some agents always upset the locals. For her plan to work, she would need their help, especially the lead detective.

"You'll take Masters."

She tried her best not to show her irritation, but failed. Smith knew her too well.

"You look just like your father when you get pissed."

She sighed. It was a problem working for a man who knew her family so well. Martin Smith had started at the FBI about the same time her father had. When her mother died, he had been the one there for them, the one to pick up the pieces. He and his wife were the closest thing she had to family. Which made it harder to conceal what she was thinking from him.

She settled down in the chair in front of his desk. "We don't get along. Other than his wife, I don't think he likes women. At least, he doesn't like me."

"You know why he's like that, why a lot of them are like

that. Every single one of them thinks you got this job because of your father's legacy. But I can't send you without an agent who doesn't know how to run a case like this. He's only going to get you started, and then he'll come back. We want this low key, just like you said. If you need help, you're to contact the Honolulu office."

She nodded. "I understand. Doesn't mean I have to like it."

He chuckled. "I didn't ask you to like it. Just do your job."

People's opinions shouldn't matter, but they did. Not to her personally. More that it made her job harder to do when no one wanted to work with her. It wouldn't change until she solved a big case. It wasn't fair because she had a good reputation from her time in vice, but that didn't seem to matter. She pushed those morbid thoughts aside and stood to leave. It would do her no good to worry about people's perceptions. "If that's all?"

"Flight's at eight tomorrow morning from National. Make sure you make it on time."

She nodded and had her hand on the doorknob.

"Maria."

She looked back over her shoulder. "Yes?"

"This could be a huge step up for you, but please, be careful. This guy isn't just smart, he's fucking dangerous. We've never had a woman on the case before, and if he finds out, he might fixate on you."

She nodded again and slipped out the door. She wanted to dance down the hall, but she decided that would be unprofessional. Instead, she went to the bathroom and leaned up against the wall and let it sink in. She was going to Hawaii, and she was going to hunt The Dom killer. Panic settled in her chest first. In the five years she'd been with the FBI, she'd had to fight her way to the top. Sure, she had to work five times as hard as the other agents to prove herself, but there were always those whispers that Big John Callahan was the reason she got her start.

She pushed away from the wall and looked at herself in the mirror. She had his nose, and his mother had always claimed, his frown. But this time, she was going to prove that Big John Callahan's daughter was more than just the memory of a beloved agent.

"Carino," Captain Akada yelled down the hall. "Need you in my office right now."

Damn. Rome had almost escaped the building without having to talk to the captain. From the time Rome had returned from a call, Akada had been locked up in his office with some suits, which was fine by Rome. Three days after finding Lisa and they had nothing more than they did before. Hell, they almost had less than with the other three killings. The bastard was getting better. Worse, Rome knew the killer was getting more infatuated with his work.

He reached the door and discovered it open. He slipped in and found three people in the room. One was, of course, the captain, the other were two dark suited, very unhappy looking people. Feds.

The man was typical of the species. Dark suit, blank expression. He looked like the kind of guy who would sell his mother to the highest bidder to gain a promotion. Short brown hair, brown eyes, and a frown. Typical. The woman, not much different, but there was something vaguely familiar about her. The suit showed nothing of her body. Her dark hair was pulled back into a tight bun at the base of her neck. When she looked in his direction, he felt like he'd been punched in the gut. He hadn't expected the luminous blue eyes or the full, pouty lips. Her skin was flawless.

"Shut the door, Carino."

He shook himself out of his stupor and did as ordered. Since the other two chairs were occupied by the feds, he leaned against the wall.

"This is Brice Masters and Maria Callahan of the FBI."

He nodded in their direction. "What does the FBI from the mainland want with Honolulu PD?"

The woman's eyes widened, but if he hadn't been watching, he wouldn't have seen it. This one was used to hiding her feelings, but what fed wasn't trained to do that? Still, there was something ice cold about her behavior, something that bothered him on a level he couldn't understand. Possibly because he couldn't read her emotions, which left him on the outside.

"They've been chasing a serial killer. The Dom. They think he might be our guy."

Of course he had heard the name. It had been splashed on every headline for the last year. He wanted to argue with them, but he knew it would be useless. When the FBI sunk their teeth into an investigation, they didn't let go until they chomped off a huge piece.

Despite that, there was a good chance this was their guy. Without any DNA, he hadn't been able to make any kind of match. Still, he knew from the crime scenes, this wasn't an amateur. This was someone who was very good at what he was doing. This one had been killing for a while.

Still, he refused to let them know what he thought. "What makes you think that?"

Masters smiled and opened his mouth, but the woman beat him to answering.

"Let me make some assumptions about your man. He picks up women at BDSM clubs. Or singles them out. No one really knows how he finds them, but they all go to the same club. Then, he beats them, sometimes tortures them, rapes them, and in the end, strangles them with a combo of a scarf and then finally manual strangulation. Their panties are missing, also. Did I get it right?"

So close it made him twitch. "A bit."

The smile she offered him didn't reach her blue eyes and was as cold as the top of Mauna Loa. "Really? I have a feeling I was spot on."

He hated her cockiness. Besides the fact that she was correct, he didn't like the premonition that was winding its way through his brain at the moment. He glanced at the captain. "Are they taking over the case?"

Akada shook his head. "No. Not officially."

He allowed for a beat of silence to go by. "In what capacity?"

"Agent Callahan, would you like to explain?"

From the look on her face, she didn't want to, but she straightened her shoulders. When she turned all her attention in his direction, he felt like he had been hit by a bolt of lightning. His body reacted without him being able to control it. She had looked at him before, but now she was concentrating on him only. Her attention had his blood heating. Her eyes were so large, so luminous, they were at odds with her clothing. There was nothing staid about the dark blue gaze she trained on him.

Even now, he couldn't seem to concentrate on what she was saying. His mind had melted the moment she'd looked directly at him. What the hell was wrong with him? It took all his power to get his head wrapped around the idea that he should be paying attention to her.

"We've gotten close to our man a few times. Of course, we don't go in right away because we usually wait for a few deaths before we try to take over. Our problem is that every time we show up on the scene, our man disappears into thin air. Well, when the former agents showed up."

The look she got from the other agent told her he wasn't happy she relayed that bit of info. She ignored him. Or pretended to. There was a slight wince after she realized what she said. Revealing the FBI was fucking things up wasn't always the smartest thing to do. They liked to pretend they were invincible.

From Rome's study, Masters was older than Callahan. Probably sent to supervise, and that wouldn't go over well with a go-getter like Callahan. Masters, for his part, didn't look happy about being there.

"So, you move in to investigate, he vanishes?" he asked, already getting a sour feeling in his stomach.

She nodded once. The gesture was familiar. There had been an agent, one of the first profilers who hunted serial killers. John Callahan. The eyes should have told him. Almost luminous blue, just like her father's.

"That can mean only one thing."

Yeah, and Rome didn't like it one bit. "He's one of you or one of us. Or someone connected to us. Someone with access to this kind of info."

Her eyebrows arched in surprise, and Rome tried not to

get pissed. He failed. The fact that she thought he wasn't smart enough to figure that out irritated him. He expected it, had dealt with it before, but for some reason it made him mad.

She moved her hands on her lap. He noticed that she didn't wear any rings, and for some odd reason, he was relieved by that. If he hadn't been that intrigued by that, he wouldn't have noticed the way her thumb tapped her leg. The movement was so slight, he would have missed it if he hadn't been paying attention. She was nervous.

"If we come in here and take over, he'll know. He has some kind of connection, whether it's through him or someone he's close to, someone he knows. Since I'm new to the case, he won't know me, won't pick up on me being here for it. But we can't let anyone know I'm with the FBI."

He studied the two of them and shook his head. "Then you better do something about the way you're dressed. Did anyone see you come in?"

She glanced at Masters then down at her own suit. When she looked up, she grimaced. "Dammit, you're probably right."

He shouldn't want to help Callahan, but something in him wanted to make sure she stayed. "We'll fix it. We can say that there was an old case from Seattle when I worked homicide there. Then you two need to assimilate."

"What does that mean?" Masters asked, but his partner was smarter.

She sighed. Rome could barely hear it, but he picked up on her irritation. "Look around, Masters. People don't wear suits here. I should have thought of it, but we came straight from the airport."

At least she was smart enough not to get pissed at him for

pointing it out. Which in his book made her smarter than the average agent. "Where are you staying?"

She didn't even allow her partner to speak. The older agent might have been sent to babysit Callahan, but she definitely saw herself in charge. "Right now, the Hilton Hawaiian Village. But we're looking for something more permanent."

Masters made a face. It was easy to see the agent didn't want to be here. Of course, it was probably more to do with who he was with. No one, not even Rome, would want to come to Hawaii with a woman who didn't know how to have fun.

"Okay. I'll meet you for drinks in the lounge right by the big pool at the Hilton."

She said nothing for a second but studied him as if he were a bug of some sort. Then, she nodded. "Time?"

"Seven."

She sighed. "Okay. Let's go, Masters."

Both of them stood, and Rome couldn't help but admire her height. He glanced at her shoes and saw that she wore low heels. She was as tall as Masters. The agents walked out the door, and it shut with an almost silent snick.

For a moment, the captain said nothing. Then he chuckled. "That was very friendly of you, Carino."

He watched Callahan and Masters walk through the squad room until they disappeared through the door. Rome shot a smile over his shoulder at his boss. "Considering who her father is, I figured I'd play nice."

"Was. Big John died about eighteen months ago. Did you know him?"

He nodded, thinking of the giant man he'd heard talk. "Went to a few of his lectures years ago when I was stationed in the DC area."

"Make sure you continue to make nice. The FBI might want to take this over, but I want to make sure that when we catch this son of a bitch, Honolulu PD gets some credit."

Rome offered his boss an angelic smile. "I promise to be a good boy."

"I didn't tell them your connection to the club, but I think you better tell her. She's pretty sharp, and if you aren't careful, you'll find yourself off the case."

He nodded and headed out the door. No matter what, he was on the case until he caught the bastard. And no one, not the FBI or the HPD, would tell him differently.

Rough Submission is releasing 3/1/2024!

about the author

From an early age, USA Today Bestselling author Melissa loved to read. When she discovered the romance genre, she started to listen to the voices in her head. After years of following her AF Major husband around, she is happy to be settled in Northern Virginia surrounded by horses, wineries, and many, many Wegmans.

Keep up with Mel, her releases, and her appearances by subscribing to her <u>NEWSLETTER</u>. If you want to keep up with cover reveals, new behind the scene info on her writing, and when new excerpts are posted, follow her MelissaSchroeder.net News News. Or you can do both! They are low traffic, so you will not get tons of emails.

Check out all her other books, family trees and other info at <u>her website!</u>
<u>If you would want contact Mel, email her at: melissa@ melissaschroeder.net</u>

instagram.com/melschro

amazon.com/author/melissa_schroeder

facebook.com/MelissaSchroederfanpage

bookbub.com/authors/melissa-schroeder

goodreads.com/Melissa_Schroeder

tiktok.com/@melissawritesromance